Totally Bound Publishi

Master Class

ENTICEMENT

SIERRA CARTWRIGHT

Enticement
ISBN # 978-1-78686-352-2
©Copyright Sierra Cartwright 2018
Cover Art by Posh Gosh ©Copyright March 2018
Interior text design by Claire Siemaszkiewicz
Totally Bound Publishing

ENTICEMENT

Dedication

For anyone who has ever loved someone who has
served in the military. YOU are my hero.

Chapter One

What the fuck?

Pierce Holden narrowed his eyes and propped a booted foot behind him on the upscale honky-tonk's wall, wondering what the hell he was watching, and why the hell it mattered to him.

Ella Gibson, his little sister's best friend, was standing at a bar-high table along with a couple of other people, leaning forward, her chin propped on her hand. Tonight, her brown hair — longer than he remembered from the last time he'd been back in Colorado for a couple of days' leave — framed her face and hung down her back.

A soft, oversized gray shirt slid from one of her shoulders, showing off her creamy skin, and her black skirt was several inches shorter than it should have been. If she bent over any farther, her ass cheeks would flash the whole world.

Why that thought bothered him, he couldn't say.

Her long, muscular legs were bare. Since it was the middle of May, she only had the barest hint of a tan. Her cowboy boots were black with hot-pink angel wings embossed on the backs of them. *Angel wings.* That was rich, when she was dressed like sin.

Randall W. Thurston, Jr. walked over to the table and offered her one of the glasses he was holding. If Pierce's guess was right, it contained whiskey. Neat. Absently, he wondered if Junior had sprung for the expensive stuff.

The two clinked their glasses together, and she smiled up at the slick attorney.

She took a sip then wrinkled her nose and shook her head.

Alcohol was never part of Pierce's approach. He liked his subs to be sober. So much so, in fact, that he made it a requirement.

Pierce tipped back the longneck bottle and took a deep drink.

From what his sister had said recently, Ella had gone through a breakup a couple of years ago. It had devastated her enough that she'd avoided dating for more than a year.

Seemed to him as if she was on track to make a full recovery.

Pierce wished she had better taste in men. He wondered if she had any inkling that Junior was a Dom. If so, and she was still talking to him, she either hadn't heard the rumors about him, or she was reckless.

From the outside, Junior appeared acceptable. The man had a fancy degree from a prestigious school. If he hadn't already made partner, no doubt the announcement was forthcoming. He wore wingtip shoes that were glossed to a military shine. Pierce would be willing to bet the man hadn't polished them himself. Maybe it was a chore he gave to a submissive. His suit was tailored and expensive. Unlike Pierce's haircut, which was the result of a once-a-week pass with his own set of clippers, Junior's hair lay perfectly, no doubt styled at an expensive salon.

The white, veneered smile couldn't hide the fact the slick lawyer had cheated on his wife and helped a man get away with murder — both sins in Pierce's structured world. None of that surprised him, though. Years ago, at a play party hosted by Joe Montrose, a good friend of his, a Dungeon Monitor had stopped a scene when Junior had refused to honor a sub's safe word.

The band trailed off, and after the applause died away, they strummed the opening notes of *Came Here to Forget*, a song that couldn't have been more apropos.

Behind Pierce, someone launched a cue at pool balls, shooting them across the green felt in an explosive boom. It was all he could do not to jump. Most men didn't have trouble blocking out the sounds of people having fun at a bar, teasing each other, calling out which pocket they were going to sink the solid into, but to him, and to countless others who'd been under heavy artillery fire, the surge of adrenaline was inevitable.

Even when he was away from combat, he was always aware, always on guard.

To calm himself, from the noise as well as the sight of Ella about to walk into dangerous territory, he took another drink of the all-American lager. Nothing fancy. Serviceable. Affordable. And with an alcohol content below that of popular microbrews.

Across the room, Junior drank his whiskey in a single swallow then slammed the empty glass down on the tabletop and signaled for the waitress.

Ella placed her barely touched drink back down and rose, lifting the heels of her boots from the scarred wooden floor as she leaned forward, her body language flirtatious, in order to catch something Junior was saying. Her leg muscles flexed in a way that appealed to Pierce's baser nature, and that damnable skirt rode up just a little more.

Fuck.

Instead of looking at her face, Junior glanced down her shirt.

Prick.

"There's something about Randall that I don't like," Morgan said, joining him.

Pierce turned toward his little sister and saw a ferocious scowl on her face. "That he's a cheat?"

"Yes. That. But it's more than that." She shrugged. "I'm not sure. Something about the way he looks at me. It's hard to explain. Like he wants to devour me. Creeps me out."

"Is Ella dating him?"

"No. At least not that I've heard. And she would have said something. He's a member of the *country club.*"

The way she looked down her nose and emphasized the last two words told him a couple of things. Junior belonged to the same club as their parents. And Morgan also believed that Junior was a pretentious ass. "Have you told Ella what you think?"

"You can bet I intend to. I don't even know what he's doing here. The Neon Moon doesn't seem like his kind of place."

"Slumming with us."

"Hard to imagine, isn't it?"

"Anyway, I need to go," she told him. "Mom and I have mani-pedis at the nail salon tomorrow morning. And I'm sure mimosas will be involved." She rolled her eyes. "God help us all."

Their mother could be dramatic at the best of times. Factor in a little alcohol and she qualified for an award.

After shaking her head, Morgan glanced back at Ella and the other people at the table. "I'll let them know I'm leaving. How about you?"

He shook his head. "Think I'll stay a while. Finish my beer."

"Are you kidding me? You're always the first one to hit the exit at these gatherings, not the last." She reached forward so that she could put her fingers on his forehead, pretending to take his temperature. "Who are you and what have you done with my brother?"

"Funny." But she was right. He left the bar scene to others. If he hadn't wanted to avoid spending time with his parents and talking about plans for tomorrow's party, which his mother hoped would make the society page, Pierce wouldn't have accepted the invitation to meet Morgan and a few of her friends at the Neon Moon—not that he'd spent much time talking to them. And until he'd seen Junior make a move on Ella, Pierce had been planning to go back to the hotel before eight, get in a quick workout, maybe a soak in the hot tub and a few minutes of mindless television. "Go home, Morgan."

"Don't forget Mom and Dad are expecting you to arrive in time to help set up tomorrow. By noon? Please?"

"I'll be there." Their parents were celebrating their thirtieth anniversary, though with the coldness with which they communicated, he had no idea how they'd made it that long. Determination, maybe. Stubbornness, for sure. And without a doubt, it was all for show.

His mother had started planning last year and had reminded him of the invitation at least once a month. A few weeks ago, she'd resorted to strategic measures and had enlisted Morgan's help. His little sister had said, "It would help me if you came." His parents, he could resist. Morgan? Never. "Twelve hundred hours," he acknowledged in military time.

"It would be easier if you just stayed at their house, you know."

In the bedroom that was part shrine and a total reminder that he'd failed to fulfill the dreams his mother and father had had for him? Last he'd been in there, a college acceptance letter still sat on the desk in mute condemnation. In his final days of high school, he'd destroyed his parents by enlisting in the army then heading to basic training without saying goodbye. "I'm fine at the hotel."

"You sure? It's a long drive."

"Less than half an hour." In military terms, that was nothing. And the small place had a hot tub to soothe his muscles and a workout area to burn off the nervous energy that built up every time he was forced to interact with his family.

"Take pity on me? I could use the buffer," she admitted.

"You've gotten everything you're going to get out of me, no matter how much I love you. But I'm happy to let you stay at the hotel with me."

"Mom would kill me."

"She'd get over it."

"I've never been as brave as you, Pierce."

"You're just easier to manipulate."

"That's not true." She wrinkled her nose. "Is that true?"

He didn't respond.

"I hate that you're right."

"Go," he said.

"Fine. See you tomorrow."

"Don't let Mom have too many mimosas," he warned. "It's going to be a long day. She needs to pace herself." He watched Morgan walk up to Ella, and Junior's smile faded at her approach.

Pierce didn't have to overhear the conversation to see Ella smile and indicate she was staying.

His sister whispered something into her ear.

Ella's back went rigid for a second. She glanced at Junior then back at Morgan. Then Ella reached across to squeeze Morgan's hand, as if reassuring her everything would be okay.

The waitress returned with another round for the table, and Morgan took that opportunity to excuse herself.

With a last wave in his direction, she left the bar.

Pierce watched Junior down his second shot, and Ella scooted her glass to the side.

The Blake Shelton song playing in the background was replaced by an older ballad. A number of couples made their way toward the parquet dance floor. Seeming to take advantage of the new intimacy in the place, Junior moved nearer to Ella and skimmed his fingers across her bare shoulder.

In Pierce's mind, a line had been crossed. An urge to protect drove him.

Junior might have helped a client get away with murder, but Pierce sure as hell wasn't allowing the creep to put his hands on Ella.

Pierce slammed his drink on a nearby table, strode toward Ella then angled his body between hers and Junior's. "Dance?" he suggested.

"I'm talking with Randall."

"Were. You were talking to him. And you're done."

She scowled. "What?"

"Dance with me."

"Do you have any idea how rude you're being?"

"As a matter of fact…" He tipped his head to one side and grinned. "Yeah. I do."

"Ella?" Randall asked, craning his head to the side.

"Now," Pierce said, refusing to budge.

"It's okay," she told Randall with a forced smile. "I promised Pierce I'd dance with him."

It shocked him how easily the lie had rolled off her tongue.

"Shall we?" With a show of male dominance, Pierce placed his fingers on the small of her back and looked at Junior, sending a *stay back* message.

Aware Randall's gaze was fixed on them, Pierce smiled. Junior loosened the tie that Pierce would have liked to choke him with and signaled for the waitress instead of talking to the other people at the table.

"What in the hell is your problem?" Ella demanded, looking up at him.

How had he never really noticed how petite she was? He'd always seen her as his little sister's friend, not as a woman in her own right. To be fair, he hadn't spent a lot of time with her since he'd moved away. In the intervening years, she'd become not only attractive, but stunning. Her hazel eyes were wide and, fuck it all, her lips were an inviting shade of red. No wonder Junior was hot for her.

Thanks to a woman he'd dated for a while, Pierce knew the basic two-step. Nothing fancy, but enough to get Ella alone and not embarrass either one of them.

He pulled her toward him. His arms fit nicely around her, despite the rigid way she held herself away from him. The overhead lights reflected off the coppery tones in her hair. And, this close, he drank in her scent, that of sunshine and promise, an intoxicating, perhaps lethal combination that he suddenly wanted to sample.

"Pierce?"

Jolted, he shook his head.

"I asked you a question," she said. "I'm not in high school anymore."

"So I've noticed."

"I don't need rescuing," she finished.

Despite her heated words, she moved flawlessly, following his lead. All of a sudden, he wondered if she'd be just as perfect in other ways, too. Rather than getting into an argument, he countered with, "What do you know about Junior?"

"Junior?" She frowned, her eyebrows drawing together. "You mean Randall?"

"Yeah."

"He'd hate it if he heard you call him that."

"I'm counting on it."

She scowled at him. "I'll ask it again. What is your problem?"

"I don't like him hitting on you."

"And?" She blinked. "What I do and who I do it with is none of your business."

"I'm making it my business."

She laughed. "Sorry to disappoint you, Pierce. You're my best friend's big brother, but that doesn't give you any right to stick your nose in my business."

"Someone has to look after you."

"No. Really. They don't. As I mentioned, I'm a big girl now. I can think for myself, choose who I want to hang out with. But thank you for your concern." She gave him a dazzling smile.

He just wished it wasn't as fake as it was big. And that it hadn't walloped him in the solar plexus. "What is it about him that you like?" he asked, again trying to keep her off balance so that she could hear what he had to say. He needed to get her past her annoyance first.

"He's a good conversationalist."

Pierce schooled his reactions so he could keep a straight face. "He must have been talking about one of his court cases. Maybe how he impressed the jury. Or found the best witnesses. Give him a spellbound audience and he'll go on for hours."

She frowned.

"He was boring you, wasn't he?" Maybe that was why she'd been shifting from foot to foot, the hem of her skirt swishing with every move. "Tell me I'm wrong," he encouraged.

For a few seconds, he watched her struggle to suppress a grin. Being diplomatic, she didn't respond to his challenge. Instead, she gave a different answer. "He's successful."

"That's easy when you get into a good law school on a legacy admission."

"Just because his dad and uncle went there doesn't mean anything."

"Oh? Any idea what his GPA was? Does he talk about that? Or the fact he had a cushy job lined up at his father's firm?"

"Okay, that's enough." She pursed her lips in what he imagined was supposed to be a fierce manner.

It just made her adorable.

"I appreciate your concern," she went on. "But I was having a good time until... Wait. Crap. Did Morgan say something to you? She doesn't like him."

"This is about me, not Morgan."

"In that case, we have nothing left to say. Thank you for the dance. I'll be getting back to Randall now." She started to pull away.

"You know he's into BDSM?"

She faltered, then she missed the next step.

Pierce pulled her close and eased her back into the dance. "So you do know." He was stunned and delighted.

But she seemed appalled. "Oh, my God. What did Morgan tell you about me?" Twin lines of scarlet embarrassment stained her face. "She promised to keep it secret."

"Is that what this is about? Do you need your ass spanked, Ella?"

"And what if I do?" Her words were laced with bravado and her eyes flashed with challenge fed by the brush of anger.

"Then I'm happy to oblige you."

"You're..." She trailed off then glanced around, as if to make sure no one was looking at them.

"Right here. Now, if you want. I can take you out back, or to my car, even to the ladies' room, if you're desperate."

"This conversation is inappropriate."

"Is it? Is that why you haven't pulled away or slapped my face?"

"I just said that you're my best friend's big brother."

"So?"

"Could you be any more obtuse?"

"Enlighten me," he said easily.

"We are so not having this conversation."

"But you are willing to have it with Junior." That thought pissed him off and tension crawled up his spine. "You know nothing about him. You're willing to let him tie you up, maybe lay a belt to your gorgeous backside."

"Okay, Pierce. Since you did so much work to get me out here, I'll play along. What do *you* know about BDSM?"

"Is that an honest question? Or are you issuing a challenge?"

She took a small breath. Her indignation seemed to have vanished. "I'm curious."

"I've practiced it for over ten years."

Her eyes widened.

"I've been to clubs, to play parties, and I own an assortment of toys that would keep even the neediest, greediest sub happy. I prefer a flogger to anything else, but I'm competent with and happy to use a cane so you can have a few marks to remember me by. Would you like that? On the backs of your thighs?"

Her breathing became shallow.

Oh, yes. No doubt the petite spitfire wanted exactly that. His arousal spiked, hard and fast. He kept her against him because having her near was so fucking right. "You could show up at my mom and dad's anniversary party tomorrow in a short dress and spend the evening wondering whether anyone could see the strokes of ecstasy that I'd seared into your skin."

She still hadn't run—she hadn't even blinked. So quietly that he had to strain to hear her above the band, she asked, "You're a Dom?"

"I answered your question. Now it's your turn. What do you know about BDSM?" Why did the thought of anyone else marking her infuriate him?

"I know enough," she replied.

"If that's true, my questions shouldn't unnerve you."

"If you were a man I was considering as a Dominant, they wouldn't," she said.

"I'm telling you this, Ella. If anyone's going to tie you up and beat you tonight, it will be me. Is that what you wanted to hear?"

"I... We can't."

"Because?"

"Beyond the obvious? You're in the military. I've had enough of men who move along when they're assigned to a new duty station."

He winced at that. His special operations team was deployed more often than most other members of the army. The assignments tended to be shorter, but also more frequent, up to six times a year. And he wasn't based in Colorado. All of which were strikes against him in her eyes, he was sure.

"I understand what you're saying." Less than a year into his military experience, he'd made the decision not to become involved in a long-term relationship. He dated casually and enjoyed scenes with subs, but he was honest about his lack of availability and his aversion to commitment.

One woman he'd cared for had been convinced they were meant to be together, and she'd expected him to change his mind, especially once mutual friends had announced their engagement. When he hadn't proposed at Christmastime, she'd given him a tearful ultimatum.

He'd held her while she'd cried, and he hadn't flinched when she'd slapped his face before leaving. That night, for the first and last time in his life, he'd gotten drunk.

Ella glanced back toward the table. Her other acquaintances were still gathered around, but Junior wasn't there. She frowned, and Pierce watched her scan the room, looking for him.

Ella noticed him a moment later. Junior was at another table, drink in hand, leaning toward a woman with his gaze focused on her chest.

Pierce hated for the fucker to hurt her, but he had to admit to being glad that she'd seen his real nature before she'd become involved with the bastard. "I'm sorry," he said.

She pasted on a sunny smile, as fake as it was brave.

The song ended. The guitarist said the next song would be a line dance. People — most of them women — abandoned their drinks and partners, grabbed a girlfriend by the wrist and headed toward the dance floor.

Since he had no interest in boot-scootin' across the floor, Pierce walked her back to the table.

Junior was still occupied, so Pierce took the man's spot.

He faced Ella, which seemed fine since the other people at the table were deep in their own conversations. "Do you want to continue our discussion here or somewhere else?"

"There's nothing to discuss." She lifted her water glass with a shaky hand and drew a sip through the straw.

But the look she sent him from beneath her lashes told him his words had gotten to her and that she was thinking about what he'd said.

Junior returned. With a scowl, he snatched up one of Ella's untouched whiskeys and gulped the shot in a single swallow.

"Want me to call you a cab?" Pierce offered.

Junior straightened his tie. "I'm fine."

"From what I've seen, you've had more than enough. The bar's going to be cutting you off. And you don't want to get picked up for drunk driving. Daddy wouldn't like it."

"Can I give you a lift?" Junior asked Ella, ignoring Pierce.

"I'll give her a ride home if she needs one," Pierce responded.

"Why don't we ask the lady?"

"Why don't we?"

They both faced Ella to see the lady's jaw was set. She drew in a deep, heavy breath. "I have my own car. I'll see myself home, thanks."

Pierce gave a feral grin. "This is where you say goodnight, Junior."

"Fuck you, Corporal Holden."

"Staff Sergeant," he corrected easily, ignoring the obvious insult. Figured the pussy needed to get in one shot to feel better about himself. Pierce didn't blame him. "Proud to serve my country so that others can sleep well at night, whether they deserve to or not."

Junior rapped his knuckles on the table twice. "I'll be in touch, Ella."

Once he was gone, she turned her furious gaze on Pierce. "I can't believe you sent him away."

"You can thank me later."

"Thank you?" she echoed. "Are you kidding me? Do you have any idea how influential his family is?"

"Doesn't concern me."

"Does anything?"

"Yeah. But not cowards like Junior, who use intimidation and coercion to get what they want. Rats who think they're above the rules." He shrugged. "Predictable in their patterns and behavior."

"Do you always live recklessly?"

"No."

"But you like danger?"

"I wouldn't say that, either."

"Then...?" She angled her head, as if she was genuinely interested in his answer.

"All my risks are calculated. It's the best way to stay alive."

The waitress hurried over with a bill and a scowl, watching as Junior walked out of the door.

"He'll take that," Ella said to the woman.

Pierce frowned as he accepted the bill. A glance at the bottom line proved the fucker had indeed sprung for the expensive shit.

"The price of chivalry," Ella said with another of those sunny smiles he was already starting to dislike.

He dug his wallet from his back pocket.

"Hope it was worth it."

"*You* are." He gave the server his credit card. "I would have paid ten times that amount to have you alone."

The server accepted with a grateful nod, pressing the card against her chest. He'd have picked up the tab, regardless. No way would he have left Ella or the hardworking server to cover someone else's bad behavior.

"So, back to the topic at hand. How much do you know about BDSM? Dabbler? Practitioner? Just curious?"

"I wanted to know more about you," she countered.

"I'll tell you anything you want to know." He paused. "But not until you answer my question."

"Uhm… I'm more than curious."

Those scarlet streaks were back on her cheeks, brighter than ever.

The music trailed off and the band announced a brief intermission, leaving the bar somewhat quiet.

She leaned toward him, obviously so they wouldn't be overheard, and his reaction was raw, unwelcome. He couldn't remember the last time he'd been this turned on. Ever since Karen had stormed out of his life, he'd channeled his energy into his job and training for marathons. "So you've had some experience," he surmised.

"The last guy I had a serious relationship with was a Dom. It was my introduction." She toyed with her straw.

"And?"

She swirled the straw around and around. He wondered if she was ever going to answer.

"Do you want me to be honest?"

"Nothing but."

She stared into the bottom of the glass before looking up. "I miss it."

"What parts?"

After glancing around to ensure others were occupied with their own conversations, she admitted, "Nothing as much as the physical contact."

"Impact play?"

"Yes." She nodded. "There's something exhilarating about being pushed, about pushing myself."

"So you *do* need a spanking."

"Pierce…"

"I'm happy to give you one."

Her mouth opened a little. He couldn't look away. That damnable, kissable red lipstick was ready to drive him off a cliff.

"I can't tell whether you're kidding or not."

"I don't say things I don't mean, Ella. Not when it's important." He met her gaze, held it. Something vibrant flared in her eyes, something that hadn't been there a few minutes ago. The spark of temptation? If so, he was ready to ignite it. "You're as safe with me as you want to be."

Chapter Two

Pierce Holden, a man she'd had a crush on for years, *was* serious. He'd looked after her and Morgan, making sure they'd arrived home safely after prom. Another night, he'd driven them home from a party when they'd been out too late. Someone had spiked the punch, something they hadn't figured out until much later in the evening when Morgan had slurred her words and Ella had burst into an uncontrollable fit of giggles. When they'd realized someone had put alcohol in their drinks, they'd been too scared to call their parents.

Every time she'd seen him, Ella had thought he was big, strong, serious, and oh-so fucking handsome. She recalled the way he'd dressed—in tight jeans, tighter T-shirts, and scarred, black boots. With his fast cars and faster motorcycles, he'd liked danger and adventure, not conformity. He'd never fit his parents' idea of the perfect son. He'd moved out of the house during his senior year in high school, worked in an automobile repair shop that his father hadn't owned, and paid his own bills.

To her, he'd been larger than life, a man who knew what he wanted and wasn't afraid to go after it.

On more than one occasion, she'd gone to bed and fantasized about him pushing her against a wall and kissing her. But he'd never been anything other than damnably, unfailingly polite.

Tonight, though…

At first, the way he'd taken charge of the situation had annoyed her. She'd been enjoying the conversation with Randall. The man was from a well-respected, old money Denver family. He was a member of the country club where she worked. And she'd heard rumors from a woman in the accounting department that he was into BDSM. So when he'd walked over to her table and offered to buy her a drink, she'd been thrilled.

But when she'd been in Pierce's arms on the dance floor, she'd been captivated by the power of his touch and his breathtaking scent, danger mixed with spice. When she'd missed a step, he'd been there, steadying her. By slow measures, her resistance had vanished.

And when she'd seen Randall flirting with the other woman and realized he'd had way too much to drink, she'd had to admit Pierce had probably been right to intervene.

He might have saved her from making a big mistake.

But she was certain that standing here talking to him might lead to an even a bigger one.

"I promise you, Ella, I will meet all of your needs. Maybe a few you don't even know you have." His deep, rich, rumbly voice sent shivers up her spine.

Erotic thoughts careened through Ella, driving her mad with excitement. The idea of him flogging her naked body flashed through her mind, impossible, and so tempting she ached to say yes, even though she shouldn't.

One-night stands and casual hookups weren't for her. She became too attached too quickly, and breakups devastated her.

Over the past two years, since she'd found out that Lance had had another girlfriend—another sub—in Killeen, Texas, Ella had concentrated on building her savings account, buying a small condo, working her way into a management position and avoiding potential hurt. Now that she was taking the first steps on the dating path, she was focused, searching for a solid, stable man and a long-term relationship that would lead to marriage. If a man showed no interest in that, she moved on after the third date.

"You were willing to tell Junior what you wanted," Pierce reminded her.

She rubbed her bare arms, trying to get rid of the sudden chill that raced through her. "He doesn't frighten me," she admitted. *At least not in the same way.* All day, every day, she dealt with men like Randall. She understood how to soothe them, inflate their egos, make them feel good. She had no clue how to deal with a man as complicated as Pierce. "You make me feel as if I've been swept up in a tornado."

He regarded her intently and she noticed the tiny grooves etched next to his blue eyes, lines that hadn't been there years before. Life experience, she knew. The result of events and challenges she could never imagine. From Morgan, Ella knew Pierce wasn't just military. He was in some special operations unit. She'd guessed it was involved with counterterrorism. And the last time Ella had asked his mother how he was doing, Mrs. Holden had smiled and offered another mimosa.

Even to his own family, he seemed to be something of a mystery.

That should be reason enough for her to stay away from him.

So why couldn't she stop looking at him?

Over the years, he'd become more hardened. He was still lean, with the physique of a swimmer or maybe a runner. He wore a short-sleeved navy T-shirt that showed his well-defined biceps. Jeans that were too soft to be new fit his thighs and hips snugly, invitingly. And his boot selection hadn't changed over the years. They were black and battle-scarred.

His dark hair was cut short, severely buzzed on the sides, a bit longer on the top...just enough for her to grab onto.

Ella blinked in a vain attempt to shove away the unwelcome thought.

He carried himself with ease, and with the confidence that came from knowing he could take care of himself and any situation he found himself in. Everything about him radiated control and determination. She had never been more flustered in her life.

The waitress returned with Pierce's credit card and the receipt, shattering the tension and allowing Ella to breathe again.

She caught a glimpse of the total amount he'd paid. Randall's whiskey had cost twenty times what she'd thought it would, and remorse ate at her. She had no right to stick Pierce with someone else's bill. "Look, Pierce. I shouldn't have done that." He added an obscene amount as a tip, and remorse morphed into guilt. "Let me pay you back." She grabbed her purse from the hook beneath the table.

He raised a hand to halt her.

"At least half?"

"I've got it."

"You didn't need to."

"I sure as hell wasn't leaving it for you."

The band took the stage again and began tuning their instruments, making conversation more difficult.

"Would you like to go somewhere quieter?" he asked. "A coffee shop? Maybe take a walk in the park? It's a nice evening."

"Are you staying with your parents?"

"No. I'm at a hotel near Parker and Arapahoe. Not too far from here, and close to Mom and Dad's."

"But not too close," she said.

He nodded.

What had happened that had caused him to leave home? And more, why had he stayed away? Was it his job or something more?

She told herself it didn't matter, shouldn't matter. But she couldn't tamp down the curiosity. "There's a Starbucks on Parker Road," she said, decision made. "I think it's open for at least another hour." It would be busy with students and couples on dates, but not too noisy to talk. On the other hand, this conversation might not be one she wanted others overhearing.

What was she thinking?

A rational part of her brain urged her to thank him for bailing her out and make an escape. Her heart thundered a warning. Adrenaline swamped her stomach in short, furious waves. All her instincts screamed that he was a man who could—would—devastate her. But sensual longing and sexual need went through her like lightning, obliterating everything else. "I also have coffee at my place."

He raised an eyebrow.

"Uhm, I mean, if you're interested."

His blue eyes flared with intensity and her insides did a flip-flop.

"Do you want me to follow you there?" he asked.

"Actually, I could use a ride."

"You told Junior you had a car."

"I lied."

"Was it your wicked plan all along to get me to drive you home?"

"What if it was, Staff Sergeant?"

"It worked." He grinned. "And you can call me Sir."

* * * *

Like everything else, the rental car suited Pierce. It was gloss black, American, all muscle and restrained power. Dozens of images flitted across the movie screen in her mind. Her naked and kneeling. Him undressing her. Her running her fingers over his chest. Him tugging his belt from its loops.

Ella shifted uncomfortably.

"Cold?" He looked at her while reaching for the temperature control.

"I'm fine." *For someone who's lost her common sense.* She was under no illusions. Pierce was suggesting a scene, nothing more. No whispered promises. But on Sunday or Monday, he'd be returning to active duty.

The only thing he was offering was the one thing she'd promised herself she'd avoid.

She told him to take a right turn, then he followed the rest of her directions and snaked the rental car through the streets until he reached her home. Fortunately, the unit next door was for sale, which meant she had no neighbors.

If he made her scream the way she was fantasizing about, that would be a good thing.

Once he'd parked, he walked around to her side to help her out. Pierce closed his hand around hers firmly, but not too tightly. He held her for a few seconds longer than necessary. The combination of his gentleness and reassurance made her apprehension vanish. She just wished her nervousness would go along with it. The idea of getting naked with a man for the first time, especially one who might be tying her up and spanking her, left her shaky.

"Everything okay?"

"Fine." Her voice was a little high-pitched.

But after a few seconds, he nodded and let her go.

Until that moment, she hadn't realized she'd stopped breathing.

"Nice place," he said as they walked up.

"Thank you. I'm rather proud of it, honestly. It's close to work and I don't have to do any of the outside maintenance." The exterior was a type of stucco, the color of red clay. Cheery blue shutters provided a homey touch that had made her fall in love with it. In a way, the contrast of colors had reminded her of a trip she'd once taken to Santa Fe. To add to the feel, she'd planted lavender in southwestern-style pots on her front porch.

She flipped on a light when they were inside, and she wondered what it looked like to him, a man who oozed solitary, masculine style.

The townhouse was two stories, with a wide-open floor plan. The focal point of the first-floor room was a fireplace. The white-painted mantel above it overflowed with framed snapshots. Some were of her with friends, others with her mother. Ella's absolute favorite—occupying the center spot—was a faded picture of her with her late father. She'd been three, sitting on his shoulders waving a flag at a hometown Fourth of July parade. He'd been smiling, and she'd been giggling. It was the last picture of them together.

The remaining space was filled with dried flowers in vases and a few vacation souvenirs, including a conch shell she'd hand-carried back from the Caribbean.

Every time Morgan visited, she complained that the living room was cluttered with too much seating, but Ella liked entertaining and having company. She had blankets and pillows stacked on the sofa and the chairs. And because she liked to read, end tables held books and magazines. Two torch-shaped lamps added atmosphere.

She had numerous potted plants in every corner and hanging from hooks in the ceilings. Almost all of her artwork highlighted the importance of family and friends, of memories and enjoying the moment. She figured now that he'd seen the inside, there was no way he could doubt how different they were.

"Nice place. Homey."

"It drives your sister crazy. Too much stuff. I'm surprised it doesn't bother you."

"After living in barracks and my spartan apartment, it's a nice change."

Surprising her even more, he moved toward the fireplace to look at her knickknacks and photos.

"Your mom?" He pointed at a photo.

"Yeah. She lives in Colorado Springs, but I don't see her as much as I'd like. She's too busy with her job, social engagements, volunteer work, that sort of thing." Ella shrugged. "I have to call her a month in advance to get on her calendar."

"Is this your dad?" He picked up the framed snapshot.

"That was a couple of months before he died in a car wreck."

"Sorry for your loss."

"Thank you." She wrapped her arms around herself. "I'm not sure people heal from something like that. Of course, we were forced to go on, but it shaped who I am, my view of the world. All of a sudden, I didn't feel as safe. But it has helped me to focus on what really matters to me."

"Relationships."

Which was another reason why a one-night stand was so difficult for her. She nodded. "And how precious every moment is. I spend as much time as I can with the people I care about."

"Did your mom remarry?"

"No. She threw herself into taking care of me, making sure I had the same kind of upbringing I would have had if Dad hadn't died. He left life insurance, but she still worked two jobs to keep the house so I didn't have to go to a new school. When I went to college, it was as if she'd been reborn. So many men, so little time. Last we talked, she was juggling three."

"Three?"

"Until recently, she was seeing four. But she broke up with the preacher."

"She was dating a preacher?"

"For a short time. It turns out they had different expectations about certain carnal things." She grinned. "She got tired of him praying for her soul. She thinks it's just fine, thank you very much."

"I like your mother already."

"She's a character. There's nothing I can't tell her."

He replaced the photo.

Ella led the way to the kitchen, and he took a seat at the granite-topped breakfast bar.

"Can I offer you coffee?" Nerves assailed her. "Or I have beer." To distract herself, she opened the refrigerator and pretended to survey the contents. "Wine? Soda?"

"Just the conversation."

"Water?"

"That'd be great. Thanks."

She grabbed two bottles, closed the fridge then turned toward him.

Pierce wore an easy grin, as if he sensed her nervousness. Her hand shook as she slid one across the countertop to him.

He nodded a thanks and set it aside, unopened.

She uncapped her bottle and swallowed a long drink. To keep much-needed distance between them, she took a few steps back to prop her hips on the counter next to the fridge.

"Tell me about your BDSM experience." His voice was half invitation, half unyielding command.

He didn't waste time. She toyed with her bottle as she answered. "The last man I was involved with, Lance, introduced me to it. We went to a few play parties, but it was an occasional, kinky kind of thing. I'd dress in leather when we went to clubs, we'd have scenes when we got home. That sort of thing."

Pierce nodded. "So you didn't live together?"

"No. He was stationed at Fort Carson, and had his own place with a couple of buddies. He'd come over maybe once during the week, and at least every other weekend." In retrospect, she realized she should have recognized the warning signs, but she'd been in love. She'd convinced herself he was busy, working hard or in the field on maneuvers. And she'd allowed herself to believe that he'd one day figure out they were meant to be together.

"Any other relationships?"

"That included BDSM? No."

"You didn't go back to play parties? Clubs?"

She shook her head.

"You told me earlier that you miss it. So why haven't you looked before now?"

"Do you have a questionnaire you'd like me to fill out?" Ella demanded.

"Just curious," he said easily. "I want to know you."

Funny. She quizzed her dates in the same way, probing, wanting to know as many details as possible in the shortest amount of time. She wasn't sure she liked being the focus of that attention, though. "No. It seemed odd for me to go by myself. The idea made me uncomfortable. I wanted to be with someone who could offer guidance." She deliberated for a couple of seconds before adding, "I talked to a couple of men online who said they were Doms. But I was never comfortable meeting them. They seemed more interested in hook-ups or exchanging kinky emails and pictures than in having a real relationship." Ella had nothing to lose by being honest with him. "I only started dating again recently. For obvious reasons, BDSM isn't something I mention when I first meet a new man."

"A real man won't be scared of your needs. If he is, he's not worth the investment of your time."

He could be right. "I went out with an accountant once," she said. "I made a joke about spanking...to gauge his interest. He dropped his butter knife on the floor of the restaurant. And then he shushed me."

"He—"

"Told me to shush." She nodded. "All the dramatics, too. Pressed a finger to his lips, just in case I hadn't understood the word. And he looked around to be sure no one else had heard me."

"I'm guessing you didn't appreciate that."

"As much as I would have enjoyed him throwing his drink in my face. Which is what he did, figuratively. I did learn that the life expectancy of a one-hundred-dollar bill is nine years. That's always good to know, right?"

Pierce smiled.

Despite the sexual tension crawling through her, she'd never enjoyed a man's company more.

"That explains why you were talking to Junior."

She nodded. "Tonight... I guess he met a client at the Neon Moon. And then when he was leaving, he saw me and recognized me from the country club."

"I know you work there."

"Morgan has a big mouth." Ella scowled. "Anyway, yeah. I figured he was safe."

"He's not."

"Could you make your dislike any more obvious?"

"What safe word do you use?" Pierce asked, rather than responding to her question.

"Stop."

"That works for you?"

She leveled her gaze at him. "I know red is more common, and if it's the safe word at a party or club, of course I'll use it. But I'm the type of woman who means *stop* when she says it."

"Respected," he acknowledged. "And for slow down?"

"I've never needed one," she admitted. "In fact..."

With seemingly never-ending patience, he waited.

Ella appreciated that Pierce made the discussion easy, with no more sexual charge than if they were discussing the weather. It made it possible for her to separate her feelings for him from the details of a potential scene. "I always wanted more."

"Did you ask for it?"

Heat crept up her face again. "Once or twice. But I guess I'm the kind of woman who tries to be grateful for what I get." Not that it had mattered in the end.

"What was it you wanted?"

"Something longer, maybe. A few times, it was over just when I was getting into it. And... There was a woman at one of the parties who talked about subspace. I wasn't sure whether she was joking or not."

"What do you think now?"

"I looked it up. A lot of people say they've achieved it. But I'm not sure I've been to the point that I had enough pain to tip me over the edge. I don't know." She searched for an explanation and came up empty. "Maybe I haven't been in a scene that lasted long enough. Or I haven't been able to empty my mind. Who knows?" She shrugged. "Or I could be lacking something."

"I doubt that." A smile tugged at his lips, and somehow that made him seem even more threatening. "But we could find out."

She slid her bottle onto the counter so she wouldn't drop it.

"Not that it should be the objective of a scene," he said. "Your satisfaction should be the goal."

"And yours?"

"Comes from seeing yours."

Without planning, the thought on the top of her mind tumbled out. "And sex?"

"Are you propositioning me?"

"No!"

"I was hoping you were."

Suddenly, she was wishing she had.

"It's up to you," he told her. "I have no expectations of sex. To me, BDSM is about the scene, the focus, the exquisite manipulation of pain so it becomes raw pleasure."

His words made her arousal spike.

"If you're agreeable..." He swept his gaze over her, taking his time, lingering.

Silently he'd reassured her of his meaning. He desired her, and whatever happened was up to her. "I don't sleep around," she told him.

"Neither do I."

She blinked. "What?"

"Surprised?"

"Flabbergasted," she admitted.

"One-night stands are awkward. I never know what to say. I hate leaving in the middle of the night. Worse, I don't want a woman getting out of my bed and finding her way home after dark. Having breakfast together is my preference, but that can lead to more intimacy."

She recalled being at a man's house years ago, and experiencing the same dreaded morning after. No toothbrush, limited makeup, a tight dress from the night before. She'd cooked him eggs and bacon when she'd have preferred granola and tea.

"I prefer to stick to scenes."

All of a sudden, ice went through her. "Do you have a girlfriend? Someone at home?"

"No. I'd never do that to her. Or to you. I've seen too damn much heartbreak to intentionally inflict it on someone else."

She raised her hand. "Recipient. Though I suspect Morgan told you that, too."

"What happened?"

Ella noticed he had neither confirmed nor denied her guess.

"I believed things were more serious than Lance did."

"Was he your Dom?"

"Yes. And it turns out he had a girlfriend in Killeen." She might as well get it all out in the open. "I'm embarrassed to admit that I missed obvious signs because I liked him and the play."

"Ouch. I'm sorry."

"It's okay. I'm wiser now. I'm grateful I found out before I invested any more time or energy into the relationship. That's my story. And since I'm being so straight with you, I do miss the scenes." *Miss them?* Obsessed about them was more like it. Last night, she'd dreamed she was being flogged. The Dom hadn't been Lance, but more of a compilation of a several men she'd seen at parties. She'd woken up horny, and using her vibrator had only given her temporary relief.

"What about you?" Ella folded her hands across her chest. "I mean... You have needs, right?"

"I masturbate."

"Lucky hand."

"I can show you how I like it done."

"Or I could watch." What the hell was it about him that removed the filter from her mouth?

"That's hot," he said. "Do you have toys that you like to use?"

She squirmed as things became more serious. "A few."

"Show me?"

"They're in my bedroom."

"You can get them or I can come with you."

"I...ah... Let me get them." She pushed away from the countertop and had to pass him to get to the stairs.

So fast that she didn't see him move, he snagged her wrist, stopping her. He turned her to face him.

"This is a good time to practice," he said.

"Practice what?"

"Proper responses." His eyes had darkened like they had in the bar when he'd taken her onto the dance floor. The softness that had been there a moment earlier had vanished, ice into vapor. "'Let me get them, Sir,' is what I want to hear."

Ella gulped for air, once again wondering what the hell she was thinking in agreeing to scene with Pierce. He was nothing like Lance. Pierce seemed much, much more serious in his approach to BDSM. And most other areas of his life, she surmised. Her voice soft and obedient, she repeated, "Let me get them, *Sir.*"

"Very nice."

Rather than releasing her, he threaded the fingers of his free hand into her hair, bunched it then eased her head back a couple of inches, nothing that hurt, but enough that she couldn't look away.

"You didn't tell me a word that means you want to slow down."

"I told you I've never needed one."

"You've never been with me."

Her knees started to buckle, but he was there, giving silent support.

"You said you wanted more from your previous Dominant. I intend to leave you satisfied. And that may mean you'll be taking more than you've ever received."

I hope. "In that case, I'll use yellow."

"Go get your toys."

Almost imperceptibly, he tightened his hand in her hair.

"Yes, Sir," she replied.

"But first, I'm going to kiss you, Ella."

"About time."

"Oh?" He raised his eyebrows and tipped his head to one side.

Though his expression was fierce, she wasn't intimidated. "About time, *Sir*," she corrected saucily.

His grip was as firm as it was intractable. "I've been wanting to do this all night. Open your mouth for me, Ella."

She wasn't sure whether she complied or whether he didn't wait, but their tongues were entwined. His was hot, searing. He sought her submission, and she gave it.

He groaned as he penetrated her deeper. Never had she been kissed like this. Pierce tasted of determination and promise that she hoped he could fulfill.

She met his kiss with desperate hunger. She'd yearned for something this intense.

Pierce released her wrist and placed his palm on her ass, nudging her up onto her toes to change the angle for a greater possession.

With her back arched, she wrapped her arms around his neck, holding on, trusting him to care for her.

The kiss was as demanding as it was stimulating...everything she could have hoped for. It had the potential to make her lose her heart if she wasn't careful.

She wondered how was she supposed to go back to an ordinary kiss — an ordinary man — after this?

Slowly, and simultaneously far, far too fast, he eased away.

Her mouth was swollen from his passion. But she wanted him with a hunger she was afraid she wouldn't be able to deny.

He took his time helping her to stand upright, and he released his grip on her hair.

It was then she realized he hadn't done anything more than kiss her. He hadn't slid his hand up her skirt, run a finger over her slick pussy or even cupped one of her breasts.

She knew he desired her. The blaze in his blue eyes was unmistakable. Instead, he was restrained.

The man had brought her to the edge then left her there. He was smart. And maddening.

"Hurry back, Ella. You've got five minutes or I'm coming up."

"Yes, Sir," she whispered. Ella was aware of his gaze on her backside as she dashed up the stairs.

Once she was inside her bedroom, her thoughts became a jumbled mess.

Aware of the clock ticking, she closed her eyes for a moment to clear her brain. After blinking a few times, she knelt to drag out a large plastic box from beneath the bed.

None of the contents had been touched since she'd played with Lance, and seeing them made her heart race.

She was getting the BDSM scene she craved, with a man she had a crush on.

The first thing she removed was a crop with a big red heart on the end. It had seemed like a fun piece when she'd bought it, but she couldn't imagine how ridiculous it might look in Pierce's strong hand.

Since he'd said he would be the one to tie her up and beat her ass, she took out two lengths of hand-spun silk rope. Then, just in case he wasn't familiar with how it worked, or preferred not to take the time it required, she selected a couple of pairs of soft handcuffs.

Then she paused and sat back on her heels.

She had a paddle with wicked holes in it.

Earlier, he'd mentioned stripes that might embarrass her at his parents' anniversary celebration. Right now, she craved some.

But the paddle wouldn't leave the kind of marks she wanted.

Though she'd had limited experience with a cane, she pulled one out of her box. It was rattan, thin, frightening. She thought about Pierce and how much she trusted him.

After drawing a breath to give her confidence, she placed it on the floor next to the rope and cuffs.

She put back the paddle, but decided to offer him the ridiculous crop.

After sliding the box back into place, she crossed to the far wall. The bottom drawer of her dresser was full of lingerie and a leather outfit she hadn't worn for several years.

Since he hadn't said anything about whether he wanted her naked or dressed, she grabbed the A-line leather skirt and matching shelf bra. Wondering what his reaction would be like, she hurried as she changed.

"One minute!" he warned.

"Yes, Sir!' she called back. Adrenaline rocketed through her.

Forcing herself to concentrate on what she was doing, she slipped her feet into a pair of tall, red stilettos, bending to adjust the ankle straps. She gathered up the toys she'd selected then gripped them tightly before taking a steadying breath and heading down the stairs.

Halfway down, she paused. Pierce was standing with his back to the fireplace, his arms crossed over his chest. His commanding presence overwhelmed her.

"Holy..." He trailed off.

Ella gripped the banister as he perused her, from her shoes, to the skirt and shelf bra.

Even across the distance, she saw his blue eyes flare with desire. "Damn. You're a lovely woman, Ella, with perfect instincts."

His approval sent shockwaves through her, leaving no doubt that her choice of outfit had been the correct one.

"Come here."

She walked toward him, her spiked heels echoing off the wooden floor.

In the time she'd been upstairs in her bedroom, he'd been busy. He'd scooted the couch and lamps back at least a couple of feet, rolled up the rug and moved it over near the back sliding door, leaving a large, open area, with the coffee table in the middle. She also noticed that he'd placed their water bottles on the mantel.

She stopped in front of him, and her pulse skittered in apprehension. "I'm not sure what to do," she admitted. She'd only been with Lance, and the BDSM had evolved over time.

"Communicate," he suggested. "Enjoy yourself. Relax with it, with me. Talk me through the toys you brought down. Lay them out on the coffee table. Tell me why you selected each item."

Ella knelt to spread out her toys, and when she looked at him, she read approval in the set of his jaw. Emboldened, she said, "I brought rope and cuffs because..."

He waited.

"Because you said if anyone was going to tie me up tonight, it would be you. Not everyone is into rope bondage, so I brought cuffs, too."

"Silk?"

She nodded.

"And the crop?"

Her whole body heated, so Ella knew she was blushing. "I know it might look ridiculous, but I kind of like the way it feels."

"Where?"

Oh, God. "On my nipples."

"Good to know." He picked it up and smacked his open palm. The sound echoed off the ceiling, making her jump. "And your pussy?"

"I've never tried that."

"You're willing to?"

"Yes." She sounded more breathless than confident.

"What are your hard limits?" he asked.

"The usual ones that are banned at parties. No permanent markings, no breaking of the skin, nothing that will send either of us to jail."

He nodded his understanding. "So tying you up and beating your ass is fine?"

Yes, please. She shuddered. "Isn't that why we're here?"

He picked up the cane, ignoring her sassy comment. "How much experience have you had with this thing?"

"Not much at all." Lightning bolts of awareness went through her. "But I'm curious."

"It's not a beginner's toy."

"But you can choose how much force to use, right?"

His lips twisted in a wry smile. "I imagine I can."

Pierce's words jolted her, reminding her of the differences in their lives. She had ordinary experiences — working, trying to buy a house, pay her bills, get ahead at work, thinking about a relationship — while he defended the country's freedom, did things he'd never talk about. *Yeah.* No doubt he could wield a cane with the intensity she might be able to tolerate. "Was that stupid to say?"

"No." He shook his head. "Whatever you want from me, I want to deliver. I like that you're trusting me." Pierce tested the cane, slowly at first.

She stared as he flicked it back and forth.

It lumbered through the atmosphere without a tremendous amount of force.

Then he moved it again and snapped his wrist.

The cane cut the air with a scary swish. She sucked in a breath and met his gaze. Handled like that, the rattan would leave a mark, sear, ache. She fucking wanted it...on her ass and on the backs of her thighs as he'd mentioned.

Transfixed, she watched him arrange a few pillows into a stack on the couch.

"Like this?" He tapped the top one a few times, without leaving an indent.

If she were smart, she would say yes.

"Or this?" This time, he let the rattan fly.

It landed with a thwack that dimpled the material.

She shivered. "Somewhere in between?"

He demonstrated again, leaving a precise line of marks across the pillow's surface.

"I should have realized that you knew what you were doing."

"A cane isn't to be treated lightly. I want you to understand that I will give you what you want. I'll warm you up, watch your reactions."

"Yes." She was already imagining.

"So beyond the obvious, what else is on your limits list?"

Ella was still staring at the rattan.

"Ella, please. Look at me. This is important."

She refocused. "I don't like to be left alone during a scene, especially if I'm in bondage. It's more upsetting than it is sexy."

"Tell me more."

"One time, Lance tied me up and left the room while he did some gaming. I think he didn't want to scene that night, but he humored me since I had asked. He didn't think he was being a jerk. It wasn't meant as punishment. He was just trying to meet my wants as well as his own. But I got a few muscle cramps."

"Were you hurt?"

"No. Pissed."

"I give you my word that I will be there for you at all times. I can't imagine needing to leave you, but if I did, it would be for a moment. And I would tell you where I was going and when I'd be back. First, I'd ensure it was okay with you and see to your comfort."

Reassured, she nodded. "Thank you."

"Anything else?"

"No humiliation. I just... I don't like to be called debasing names." She couldn't find the words to help him understand.

"You don't need a reason. You just need to tell me the rules."

"It's a hard limit."

He dropped the cane onto a couch cushion before taking two steps toward her and offering his hand.

She slid hers into his, feminine to masculine. Trust to strength.

"Humiliation isn't something I'm into. I think you are too perfect, too precious to debase in any way." He didn't release her. "If it were your kink, we would have negotiated something to ensure I got you off. But honestly, Ella? It would have been one of the most difficult things I'd ever done."

Damn. She so wished this could last more than one weekend. Wished he wasn't military. Wished she was the type of woman who wouldn't be hurt when he walked away.

"Just for clarity, are gags humiliating for you?"

"I've never been gagged."

"Are you willing to try?"

"As long as we have a safe signal, yes."

"Understood." He nodded. "Anything else you want me to know?"

"I'm willing to have sex with you, Sir. If you want to. I have condoms in the master bathroom, under the sink." She couldn't believe she'd admitted it. Couldn't believe how much she wanted it. Pierce and his quiet, relentless strength had gotten to her, chasing away her normal doubts and inhibitions. He was the devil incarnate. And she was ready to book a one-way ticket to hell.

Chapter Three

Pierce had meant it when he'd said that Ella was perfect.

To him, she was. More innocent than she'd like him to believe. Beautiful. Sassy. Brave. And with a dose of sexual appeal that walloped his senses.

Over the years, he'd played with a lot of women. They'd all been experienced in BDSM and, like him, knew what they wanted. He'd never made promises or created false expectations.

But because of who Ella was and what she was risking, he was doubly conscious of the weight of his responsibility to her.

He intended to give her everything she craved. All while protecting her. "Show me your body. I want to know every inch of it, where you're sensitive, and how you like to be touched." He released her hand. "We'll start with your breasts."

She locked her gaze on his as she pushed her breasts together.

"How do you like your nipples to be touched?"

Her breaths came in rapid bursts and her hazel eyes darkened.

She stroked her thumbs across her nipples, and they hardened, the rose color deepening.

"Do you like it this gentle?" he asked.

"No." She took his hands and put them on her breasts. "More," she whispered. It wasn't a demand, but a soft, sensual request.

He increased the pressure until she sucked in a breath. "How's that?"

"Enough to make me horny," she said.

The admission was more direct than he'd expected, and it made him grin. Damn, he liked learning about her.

He rolled each of her nipples back and forth, using a bit more pressure each time.

She curved her hands around his wrists. Then she closed her eyes.

He kept a close, close watch on her while he squeezed each tip.

She bent her knees and leaned toward him for support.

"You do like nipple play," he mused, easing his grip.

"I had no idea I could like it this much."

"Then I think it's time you showed me your pussy."

Her nostrils flared, and the tremble that went through her might have been missed by someone who wasn't paying attention.

"Lie on the coffee table." He cleared away the toys. "On your back." She uncurled her fingers and he asked, "Did you wear panties, Ella?"

"I guess you'll find out. Sir."

He moved quickly, taking a seat on the couch, snagging her wrist then tugging her over his lap

She squealed, more from shock than fright, he imagined.

Ella pushed her fingers against the hardwood flooring to keep her balance.

He clamped one arm across her back to hold her steady, and he raised his knees a couple of inches to tip her toward him so she wouldn't fall.

Her hair trailed wildly, the copper highlights like flames. Her skirt rode up, exposing her thighs. And those shoes — bright red — seemed to be an invitation to fuck. He was man enough to know he'd masturbate to this image a dozen times, maybe more.

"Damn, woman. If I had ever seen you like this when I'd been home on leave, I'm afraid my army career would have been over."

"AWOL?"

"Most definitely."

She gave a sound that was part giggle, part triumph.

"Vixen."

"Am I wearing panties, Sir?"

"You like to live on the knife-edge, delicious little sub?" With the way she'd behaved at the club, sticking him with a three-figure bar tab, it shouldn't have surprised him that she was a bit of a tease. Her sassy personality was a bonus, but that sure as hell didn't mean he'd let her conduct pass unpunished.

He flipped up her skirt.

She was bare.

No panties, no pubic hair. Waxed. And slick. He knew that without even touching her. *Fuck.*

This woman…

His woman…

"How many spanks do you deserve?" He rubbed her skin. "Not just for your sass, but for distracting me from exploring your body?"

"You are exploring," she pointed out. "Sir. And I think the punishment should be mitigated by the fact I'm not wearing panties."

"You do, do you?"

"If Sir's hard dick pressing against his sub's tummy is any indication, he's not terribly disappointed." She squirmed beneath his touch. "If the sub may be bold enough to say so."

"She may not."

"Oops."

"Spread your legs."

Instantly, she complied.

"Farther. Turn your toes in. In the absence of any other instruction, always assume that's my wish. How are you with anal?"

"What?" She tried to wriggle onto her side to look at him. "Now?"

"As pleasure. As punishment."

Ella tightened her ass cheeks.

"You didn't list it as a hard limit."

She didn't respond right away.

"I'll take that as agreement, then?"

"I'm not sure about the punishment part. But maybe for pleasure."

"Do you own a butt plug?"

"No."

"That answer was a little too fast."

"Well… A small one."

"You've added a few strokes for the lie, Ella." Damn, she delighted him.

He teased her pussy, stroking her labia. She dug her toes into the floor, lifting her hips, trying to influence him.

"Ella. Ella. I know what you're doing."

She stilled immediately and he pulled his hand away. "Go get the toy. Bring some lube, too, and I'll consider whether or not I'll use it when I shove the plug up you."

She crossed her legs.

"That's not turning your toes in," he said. He dropped his knees and helped her to stand.

"Sir…"

"The plug, Ella."

"Yes, Sir," she mewled.

He watched as she walked up the stairs, taking her own sweet time, exaggerating the sway of her hips.

When he'd agreed to Morgan's desperate pleas for him to come home for the weekend, he hadn't been expecting this. He might accept a few more of his pesky sister's invitations after tonight.

Ella moved around upstairs, and it seemed she was taking more time than necessary. "If you touch that pussy, I will cuff your hands for the rest of the night!"

She called something back. It might have been, "Yes, Sir." But it easily could have been something else.

Within a minute, she was standing in front of him. The slender piece of silicone wasn't much thicker than his forefinger. It would do. For now.

He extended his palm and she gave him the requested items.

"Are you—?"

"Over my lap."

She looked at him.

He raised his eyebrows. "Do you need me to repeat my order?"

"No, Sir."

She stared at the plug for a few seconds before doing as he'd asked.

"We'll continue the exploration of your body," he said. "Reach back and spread your buttocks."

"I'll fall."

"I won't let you." He put his free palm flat against the middle of her back.

"It's been a long time since I did anal," she said.

"If you want me to use lube, you'd better do as you're told and quit stalling."

She lifted her hands from the floor for a couple of seconds, but then she quickly dropped them again.

Pierce waited.

Then she reached behind her with a little more confidence and spread her cheeks, giving him a glimpse of her tiny, tight anal whorl.

"I'm going to keep this in you for the rest of the night," he warned. "Not all physical punishments are about spanking."

"I was afraid of that."

He waited.

"Sir," she added in a faint whisper.

He reached for the lube, flipped the top then drizzled the viscous liquid over the plug. "Relax as much as possible," he informed her. "It's going in, and it's up to you how much of a struggle it is. Bear down." He pressed the tip against her hole.

"I..."

"It's a third of the way in already." He pulled it back a little until she drew a breath, then he pressed forward again.

As the thicker part of it started to breach her, he fucked her with it, creating a rhythm she could cope with but with the progress he wanted.

"This sucks," she protested. "I don't remember it being this uncomfortable."

"Good."

"What?" She moved around, and he took the advantage to sink the toy all the way in.

She yelped.

"You're there." Pierce settled the base between her cheeks. "I like the way it looks. I think I'll make you wear it to my parents' party tomorrow."

"You wouldn't."

"Yeah. That settles it. And a short skirt or dress."

"What have I gotten myself into?"

"I'm rather enjoying it."

"Because you're diabolical."

"Getting more so by the minute. I want you face up on the coffee table." He helped her to stand.

"I thought…"

"That you'd get rewarded with an orgasm?"

She scowled at him.

"I've got a dozen planned for you. How many of them you receive is up to you."

"Is this my incentive to behave?"

"I don't know." He lifted a shoulder. "Is it?" Either way, he was fine with it. He enjoyed being inventive with her punishments almost as much as he liked playing with her to begin with.

He went into the kitchen to wash his hands, aware of her gentle sounds behind him as she moved the toys to the couch and got into position.

When he returned, she looked exactly as he'd envisioned. Her feet were on the floor, her hands dangling at her sides, her tangled hair in that wild mess, her eyes wide, mouth parted, chest rising and falling in shallow bursts, her nipples hard and begging.

In this position, she was open to him, vulnerable. Perfect and compliant. Almost as good as actual bondage. "Show me your pussy."

"Yes, Sir." She brought her hands forward and spread her labia.

"Touch yourself."

Ella dipped a finger into her pussy then circled her clit.

He loved watching the nub swell and turn a dusty pink color. "Keep going."

With a soft moan, she closed her eyes.

"More. Give me a show."

After a few seconds, she began to move her hips. She made faster, tighter circles on her clit. Her breathing became more erratic.

He let her continue until she lifted her hips, tightened her buttocks and slid a finger inside herself. "That's enough."

She pursed her lips but didn't protest. Nor did she move her hand. "Ella," he warned.

"Just a minute. I've been out of my mind since we were at the Neon Moon."

"I said stop."

"But, Sir…"

Pierce could smell her arousal. Was there anything sexier than a woman waiting for a man to pleasure her? "Is there a reason you're being a deliberately disobedient sub?"

That got through to her. She froze and opened her eyes.

"That's better. Now let your arms drop to your sides."

Ella sighed.

With her body exposed and her breaths even, he took a couple of steps toward her then bent over to stroke between her folds.

With a keening moan, she arched toward him.

"So your clitoris doesn't need as much stimulation as your nipples?"

"Not at all. But since I was touching myself, I'm already aroused."

He pressed his thumb to her clit while sliding a finger inside her wet cunt. "And this... Is this what you want?"

"Oh."

"Oh?"

"Yes. Yes, Sir. That's what I want. Thank you."

Her pussy clenched around his finger. Because of the plug in her ass, she was tight, and he was certain that had to make his movements more invasive.

How long had it been since he'd been with a woman this responsive? If he wasn't careful, he might become addicted.

She fisted her hands.

"How close are you to an orgasm?"

"Seconds, Sir."

He moved his thumb even faster and inserted a second finger then started fucking her hard. "Wait for my permission."

"I... No. That's not—"

"Wait." He touched a finger to her G-spot and saw her lift off her heels, silently demanding more.

"Sir!"

"You may come."

His woman—his sub—convulsed. She screamed, arching, seeking. Pierce watched, giving her what she needed until her shoulders relaxed again. Then he took his hand away from her. "I think I've learned a few things about you," he said. "And you've earned more of those orgasms. Now we can play."

"Now?" Ella repeated. Her body had never been more soft or supple, and her mind was at peace in a way it hadn't been since Lance had broken up with her. "Then I'm not sure what it is that we have been doing, Sir." She was already so content she'd be happy to snuggle into his arms. Maybe they could make love before they drifted off to sleep.

"Ella, I haven't even started with you."

His face appeared more relaxed than it had earlier. Tension was no longer grooved next to his eyes. It seemed he'd shut out everything but her.

Pierce picked up the cuffs. She wrinkled her nose. "I don't think I'm going to like this."

"Maybe you will." He took his time securing her wrists. As she'd come to expect, he double-checked that the bonds weren't too tight and that her shoulders were comfortable. Then he attached the cuffs to her ankles. "Damn. These shoes..."

She suppressed her grin.

With his thumb, he made a tiny circle on her right ankle. "I may take them back to North Carolina with me."

"And masturbate to the sight of them, Sir? Remembering me?"

"Ella, there'd be no forgetting you. Ever."

He secured her feet to the coffee table legs.

She lay there, a bit uncomfortable and helpless. There was nothing more thrilling than being this man's captive.

His motions exquisite and tender, Pierce rubbed her breasts and her tummy before flipping the hem of her skirt out of the way so that her thighs were exposed.

She watched him intently, fascinated by the way he studied her. His deliberateness ignited her senses.

Then he picked up the crop.

Ella had been afraid it might appear ridiculous in his masculine hand, but it didn't.

Then she noticed his gaze was focused on her pussy. "Uhm, you can't mean to use that on my "

"Pussy?" he supplied.

The pretty bright red heart had seemed fun at the store, but now it terrified her. "I'd meant for you to use it on my butt, Sir." Someplace where there was plenty of padding.

"I'm sure you did."

He stood over her and trailed the edge of the heart down her chest then over her belly before dipping between her legs.

Ella tried to keep still and failed. Even though she'd just orgasmed, her nerve endings reignited. She'd never been with a man who understood her or her body this well.

He tapped her breasts, her nipples, her legs, her pussy. Terror vanished as if it had never been there. "Oh..."

Then he smacked the inside of her thigh hard. It didn't burn — it was a dull, achy, fabulous thud.

He caught her again, on the other thigh.

Before she was ready, he brought it down on her already-throbbing pussy. She screamed, clenched her ass cheeks — making the silicone shift inside her — then thrust her pelvis forward, offering her body...her trust.

"*More.*"

"That's a perfect response."

The hurt had been exquisite, maybe because he'd already tormented her pussy so much.

He moved on to her breasts, cropping them, hitting her nipples, making her tremble with the need to come again. Pierce rained kisses of torment down her belly, then again between her legs, not just her clit, but all of the exposed, sensitive flesh.

"What do you want?"

"My clit," she pleaded.

"Be clear."

"Spank my clit with the crop, Sir." She couldn't believe she'd asked for that. Couldn't believe how much she needed it.

"How many times? Just once?" He tapped her lightly.

"Sir!" Frustrating. Maddening. She looked up at him, but he wasn't watching her face, he was focused on her pussy.

"How many, sub?"

"Five, Sir? Six?" *A dozen.*

Just when she was afraid he wouldn't give her what she had been begging for, he parted her labia.

Common sense urged her to backtrack, tell him she'd changed her mind. But raw desire crowded every thought from her brain. "Do it."

Pierce lowered the heart then pulled back and gave her a stinging slap.

She yelled. It burned. It stung. And she ached with the need to come. "Pierce. Sir. Sir, sir, sir."

"Your pussy is bright red, swollen."

"I need…"

He placed the crop on her stomach then crouched to lick away the pain, soothing her, driving her mad.

Tension coiled in her body. "I have to come."

All of a sudden, he stopped.

"What?" She shook her head and pulled against the restraints. "Sir?"

"I like having you this aroused."

"You can't leave me like this."

"No? Having you on the edge will make it easier for you to take the cane marks that I intend to give you."

Cane? Fear wound through the arousal, making her vibrantly alive.

"It's a kindness, if you want to think of it that way." After he released each cuff, he took a few seconds to rub her skin to ensure her circulation was fine.

"Everything's fine. Except for the fact I'm stuffed full of a plug and I need to come."

"You said you didn't have a gag?"

She clamped her mouth shut.

He grinned.

"Let's go upstairs." He offered a hand, and she accepted it.

Even just a few minutes on the wooden surface had left her a little sore.

He picked up the toys and the water bottles before following her up the stairs. The unnaturally high heels forced her to be careful. Between them and the plug he'd mercilessly shoved up her ass, her movements were slow and somewhat exaggerated. She'd never been more aware of being a submissive, never been more aware of her femininity.

This experience was so much more than she could have ever imagined.

"Condoms?" he asked when they reached the bedroom.

"I'll get them." She hurried into the bathroom. Unsure how many he'd need—just one? Two?—she decided to grab the whole box.

He was sitting on the foot of the bed, arms folded.

After placing the box on a nightstand, she stood in front of him.

"Strip for me," he said. "But leave the shoes on."

"You definitely have a thing for them."

"Wasn't joking that I might take them home." There was no teasing in his voice.

Ella reached behind her to unhook the shelf bra. She would have let it fall to the floor, but he reached out a hand to catch it.

Then she unzipped the skirt. She shimmied her hips and the material dropped to the carpet. Then, being bold, she hooked it with her shoe and lifted it.

He took the skirt from her foot. "You'll be the death of me."

Maybe they could meet in hell.

"How does your pussy feel?"

"You had to mention it," she replied.

"And your tight little butthole? In fact, don't answer. Spread your legs then bend over and grab your ankles." He moved behind her. "Let me see for myself."

Pierce, relentless and dominant, pushed on the base of the plug. She grunted in an unladylike way and grasped her ankles tighter so she didn't topple over.

"Looks gorgeous." He turned it back and forth several times, like a corkscrew inside her.

She gasped. It hurt, and at the same time was erotic.

"You may stand."

Even as she did, he stroked his fingers over her pussy.

She clenched, on the verge of an orgasm again.

"Turn toward me."

When she did, he tweaked her nipples, much, much harder than he had earlier, and she cried out. It wasn't so much from the pain as the shockwaves of awareness.

Just when she was ready to plead with him to release her or let her come, he dropped his hands. "Sir..."

"I want you face down on the bed, Ella."

He picked up one of the lengths of silk.

"Wrists crossed above your head."

"Yes, Sir." Her heart doing a slow thud, she crawled onto the bed and into position.

"I'm going to tie you up," he said. "And give you eight strokes with the cane. You might not think you can endure. But you can. You will. And the reward you earn will make you so damn proud."

Ella buried her face in the mattress. She wanted it every bit as much as it terrified her.

Expertly, he tied the rope, ensuring it wasn't too tight and that she couldn't pull free.

"What's your word for slow?" he asked again.

"Yellow." And before he could prompt her again, she added, "And stop is my safe word."

The mattress sank under his weight as he sat next to her.

He ran his fingers down her spine, between her cheeks, across the backs of her knees.

Then he secured her feet. Unable to resist, she tested his work, pulling, wriggling.

He said nothing.

"I didn't need to worry about your competency with the rope."

"Ella, I know at least twenty ways to tie a knot so that you can't get away, no matter the material—silk, hemp, bamboo, nylon. In a pinch, I can use a pair of your stockings. And I'd be willing to bet I could figure out how to keep you in place with just your pretty bra."

"What other mad skills do you have, Sir?"

"Let's find out."

She thought he might begin right away, but she realized she should have known better. He paced himself, refusing to rush.

He smoothed his hands over her skin before rubbing vigorously. He massaged her deeply, and she knew it was to ensure a good blood flow. No doubt the man was a master at what he did.

"I know you're not all that experienced and it's been a while since you've played, I'm going to give you a few warm-up taps. They won't count toward the eight strokes I promised you."

"Yes, Sir."

As he delivered the first few, she exhaled. She'd suspected he would know how to use the cane, but this exceeded her expectations.

They weren't as hard as she'd feared they might be, but much harder than she'd anticipated.

"When the caning begins, none of the marks will be a third more harsh than the previous one. To manage it, breathe. Remind yourself you wanted it. Surrender. To the extent possible, keep your fists unclenched, your fingers spread, your body relaxed. Going through an ordeal is ninety percent mental. Perhaps more."

"Is that something you have experience with?" she asked. "From your military training?"

"It's about the story in our heads, Ella. If we are convinced we can't do something, then it will never happen. On a forty miler — that's what we call a forty-mile march — you concentrate on each step, not the entire journey, otherwise the pack, no matter the weight, would be unbearable."

She nodded then moved around, getting more comfortable, preparing herself.

"You're delectable, Ella. I love this sight of you. Bound, exposed, hot for me. If you were mine, I'd keep you like this as often as possible."

Sincerity laced his words, filling her.

"The caning is about to begin. Eight strokes. None a third more intense than the previous one."

She swallowed the sudden lump of fear that had formed in her throat.

"Ready?"

"Yes." She drew a steadying breath. "Yes, Sir."

A frightening whistle rent the air hundredths of a second before the rattan marked her right ass cheek. "Oh my God!"

The pain went on and on, radiating, getting more intense.

She squirmed, trying to get away, but from what, she didn't know.

"Gorgeous." He rubbed the ache, and it began to fade. "That was one," he said.

There were seven more to go?

He grabbed a handful of her left butt cheek and squeezed tight. Then, as soon as he let go, he seared her with another stroke.

Her body went rigid.

Just like it had last time, the pain worsened, going on and on. It was relentless, eating at her resolve. After about thirty seconds, the agony vanished, leaving behind a satisfied glow inside her. Damn it. She liked that.

He worked his hand beneath her pelvis then found her clit and began to tease her.

"Oh, Sir!" Between the pain from the stripes and the way she was already aroused, prickles of sensation rushed through her.

"You'll get a second orgasm," he promised as he removed his hand.

She whimpered.

"You have to earn it. As I told you, your pride will make it all the more spectacular."

This time, he laid the cane across both of her butt cheeks.

Ella screamed.

He gave her no time to recover. Instead, he placed another just below it and an additional one above it.

Desperate, aching, she gyrated her hips against the bedsheet, seeking to get away, hoping to grind out a forbidden climax.

"You've got three more, my brave little sub."

Could she do it? Did she want to?

Earlier she'd bravely—maybe brazenly—told him that she'd never come close to needing a word for slow down. That she wanted to be pushed. This was testing everything she had—her reserve, resolve, determination.

He worked his hand beneath her again and zeroed in on her clit. He teased her then slid two fingers inside her hot pussy.

Moaning, she tried to lift her body to give him greater access, but the bonds kept her from gaining any leverage.

Pierce thrust his fingers in and out. "You are so fucking wet, Ella."

The pain from his stripes morphed into need—clawing and consuming.

"The next ones will be harder to take," he warned. "I'll give you those marks you want, and they will be a testament to your bravery. Then tomorrow at the anniversary party, you'll show them to me."

And if they left her that far out of her mind, she wanted it.

"Cry. Moan. Scream. Curse. Whatever you need. Unless you're at yellow?"

A few minutes ago, she might have been. But now... "The way you're tormenting me makes me believe I can take anything."

"Would you like a gag?"

She shifted. "Do you want me to have one?"

"I prefer the sound of your screams to silence."

"Then no, Sir."

"Get to eight, wear my stripes, and I will reward you," he whispered into her ear.

She turned her head to meet his gaze, gaining strength from the depths of his glacial blue eyes. Oh, she wanted what he was offering, all of it and even more. She'd made her decision about sex, even if she had to suffer the emotional consequences later. "I want you to fuck me, Sir," she said.

"Now?" He frowned. "Are you stopping?"

"No."

"So me fucking you is the reward you want?" He feathered across her clit without using enough pressure to get her off.

She'd never been more sexually frustrated than she was in this instant. "Yes."

Adding to the frustration, he stopped toying with her. He plowed his hand into her hair and tightened his fist, pulling her head back enough that he could kiss her, fast and hard, heating her mouth, making her taste his power.

He completed her. Owned her.

"Your responses make me happy."

Slowly, he released his grip.

She inhaled. Tonight...this...Pierce... It was everything she could have hoped for. And more. "Please finish the caning, Sir."

"Nothing would make me happier."

He rubbed her thighs, giving her a clue of his intention.

Ella steadied her breathing and tried to keep her muscles relaxed.

"That's it."

He arched downward, caning her in the middle of her right leg. The tip seemed to bite in.

She screamed, undone by the radiating pain. "Fuck!"

Pierce smoothed his palm across the mark and the heat began to dissipate.

Before she'd finished processing the pain, he repeated the stroke, with the same kind of precision, on the other leg.

Despite all her intentions, tears filled her eyes. She laced her fingers together, trying distract herself. "Pierce, I..."

"One more. The choice is yours, though. Would you like to stop? I will adore and appreciate you no matter your decision."

"No." God, her voice ached from the anguish, filled with tears. "I want it." She had to know. She wasn't doing it for him, but for her.

His hands were on her, all over—her legs, the backs of her knees, her buttocks, her shoulders. He massaged and soothed. And all of it promised a completion that she had to have. She'd never be satisfied if he ended it here.

"Last one. No more than thirty percent harder than the previous one," he repeated.

Again the cane tore through the air before searing her as it landed well below her buttocks.

With a scream, she bucked. The motion forced her sensitized pussy against the bedding, and an orgasm clawed at her. "Pierce. Sir!"

"I've got you, Ella. I've got you." It took him less than thirty seconds to unfasten her ankles, and he spread her legs apart.

He pulled the plug out a little and fucked her with it. It was too, too much. And at the same time, it wasn't enough.

Pierce sank two fingers into her now-saturated pussy. At the same time, he grabbed the silicone by the hilt so he could pound both of her holes.

"Orgasm any time you're ready."

The pain, the sound of the cane and her emotional response to his brilliant dominance overwhelmed her

Sobbing, she shattered completely, the climax obliterating her.

"You're so perfect." He soothed her with his words, with his touch, and with a kiss on the top of her head.

Then... It was over.

She was somewhere else.

"Ella?"

She blinked, and everything around her wore a silvery, shimmery halo. Exhausted, she yawned, then she closed her eyes, surrendering to the feeling of bliss. Every part of her throbbed.

"How're you doing?"

Pierce's voice reached her as if from a great distance. Even then, it sounded fierce and protective, something she could rely on.

He moved his knuckles across her cheekbone.

Startled from the floating sensation, she opened her eyes.

"Welcome back."

She was in his lap, snuggled up to him, one side of her face nestled into his soft T-shirt. Without her awareness, he'd managed to untie her wrists, plump the pillows, remove his boots and sit on the bed, legs stretched out. "Uhm...what?"

"Subspace?" He smoothed her hair.

With a hand on his chest, she pushed away so she could look at him.

Pierce shrugged.

"Do you think?" She wrinkled her nose. "That's not what I expected. I guess I thought that was something that happened while you were being flogged or beaten. Endorphins, like a runner's high."

"The caning was substantial."

"And so was the orgasm."

"You're welcome." He grinned, and it was so disarming that she smiled back, more satisfied than she remembered being in a long time.

"We could do it again to test your theory," she suggested. "See if I can reach it again."

"Are you brave? Or reckless?"

"Both?" She settled again, enjoying the reassuring pounding of his heart. "That was nice."

"Nice?" His lips twitched. "If that's all it was to you, I'm going to have to work on my skill set."

She laughed. "Nice is good."

"Good?" he said, sounding even more scandalized.

"Fabulous, even."

"We're getting somewhere."

"Spectacular."

His arms were loose around her, but the bond was tight enough to keep her in place. She loved it. The caning had been more wicked than anything she'd ever endured. True to his promises, with his approval and encouragement, he'd made each stroke manageable.

When she imagined a perfect Dom, he behaved like Pierce had. It would be so easy to fall for him, or at least this part of him.

Ella told herself to separate her emotions from reality. They had agreed to one night together, then he'd be leaving again. God knew how long it would be until she heard from him again. *If* she heard from him again. That thought crashed into her and she forced herself to refocus. She could worry about that tomorrow. Right now, she wanted to experience everything she could. "You promised me sex," she reminded him.

"I did, didn't I?"

She crawled from his lap. "Should I undress you?"

"Was that a hint that you would like me to hurry?"

"Well..."

He climbed from the bed and stripped off his shirt in a single, upward motion.

Holy hell. From his strength, she'd known he was in shape, but she'd had no idea how honed his muscles were. His abs were hard and flat. He was lean. Rugged. Capable. He had a frightening, jagged scar on his left side, below his ribs. She shook her head to clear it. Just another reminder of what he did for a living and of her earlier, internal warning to avoid getting involved with military men.

He removed his belt, jeans and socks and stood in front of her wearing nothing but tight, navy-colored boxer briefs.

She couldn't look away.

He pulled off his underwear, and the size of his cock made her eyes widen.

"Well, Sir."

"Well, sub?"

Meticulously, he picked up his clothes and placed them in the order he would re-dress.

He donned a condom then said, "Come here."

Long and enticingly, he kissed her. Within seconds, she was hungry for him all over again.

She stroked his dick and he moaned in response.

"I've got to have you."

Ella wanted him every bit as fiercely. "Yes."

As she was coming to expect, with him being such a considerate lover, he made sure she was on the verge of coming before ordering, "I want you on the edge of the bed, with your knees as far apart as possible."

"Sir?"

"I'll show you."

He helped her into position, her ass lifted high, face on the mattress.

"Is this a yoga position I've never heard of?" she asked, afraid of losing her balance, hyperaware of the plug and the fact he'd be able to penetrate her deeply.

"Yeah. I call it the Holden Reverse Half Squat. You might want to practice it daily."

"Is that a threat, Sir?"

"It might be, if you don't do as you're told." Adding emphasis to his words, he smacked her right butt cheek.

"Ouch!" She tried to move away, but he trapped her hips.

"Behave." He adjusted her position slightly, leaving her ass and pussy even more exposed. "Cross your wrists."

Once she had, he clamped his hands over them, pinning her in place.

"I'm going to fuck you from behind so I can look at my marks on you."

Ella wanted him to be as proud of her as she was of herself. "Do me."

His thick cockhead pressed against her entrance.

She looked back but couldn't see him. She was helpless... He could do as he wished, and she shivered deliciously. "Sir."

Chapter Four

Pierce traced his thumbnail over the startling red cane mark on her right ass cheek. Nothing left a stripe like rattan. The sight of it on her delectable, creamy flesh thrilled him.

Ella wanted to please him, and that had made their scene all the more spectacular. He'd watched her every movement, calculated the mental and physical cost of each thing he did to her, wanting to give her the BDSM experience she craved.

And in return, for the first time in his memory, a woman had sneaked past his defenses.

"Sir?"

"Admiring my handiwork." It was the first excuse he'd been able to find.

"I think I will get to enjoy it for the next few days. Something to remember you by."

Her reminder that this was temporary gave him an unwelcome jolt. He wondered if she'd said it on purpose to keep her emotions safe, or whether she meant it more as a warning to him.

Responding, he kept things as light as she had. "One should hope you don't forget me or the caning anytime soon, sub."

"Fuck me, Sir. Please."

He curled his hand around his sheathed cock and teased her still-heated cunt with it. Since the plug was in, the fit would be tight.

Pierce bent his knees in order to slide in a little deeper.

"Yes," she whispered.

He stroked in and out, his cock ready to burst.

This woman, accommodating and challenging, was a joy to fuck.

Finally, hunger driving him, he sank his dick all the way in.

She expelled her breath in a rush.

"Are you doing okay?" Her strength surprised him. No doubt, she was the type of woman he needed to be with.

"Fine."

"Good. Then keep your hands in place." He released his cock to grasp her hips and imprison her.

He slid in and out slowly, repeating the process dozens of times before he shortened the strokes.

"I think you're too big."

"It's just right." He dipped a hand between her legs to heighten her arousal, wanting her to have at least one more orgasm.

"So damn full," she said, voice muffled.

So freaking tight. He wasn't sure how long he could hold off.

Schooling himself, he shook his head and withdrew his cock.

"Sir?"

"I want to look at you."

He rolled her onto her back. "Put your legs on my shoulders."

"And this is the...?"

"Holden Salutation."

She grinned and propped her feet on his chest. "Gonna need some help with this one, big boy," she teased.

Fun. That was something unique to her, making it unlike any other sex he'd ever had.

He lifted each of her legs and placed her calves on his shoulders. The spiked heels added an element of risk that he enjoyed.

After placing his cock at her entrance again, he surged forward, sliding in.

She yelped. "I think you'd better rename this one the Holden Holy Hell position."

"No worries. We'll practice until you get it." He placed an arm across her knees and saw that her hands were curved into the bedding.

Her eyes drifted closed as she gave herself over to him.

He leaned forward to play with her nipples, then moved upward to run a finger across her bottom lip, wanting her to know how much he appreciated her.

"Oh, Sir."

"Go ahead and take it."

Her pussy pulsed and he gritted his teeth to avoid ejaculating that instant. She used his shoulders for leverage to change the angle slightly.

She opened her eyes when she came, and he liked the way heated cognac seemed to spill across the hazel.

It — *she* — could become an addiction.

After she'd ridden out her orgasm, he allowed himself to climax, a sensation that seemed to come from the depths of his balls, emptying them in a satisfying way that masturbation never could.

A final shudder nearly toppled him and he shook his head.

By slow measures, he eased himself from her pussy. "Bend your legs." Before she could protest, he plucked the plug from her ass.

She sucked in a deep breath.

He walked to the bathroom, cleaned up, then returned to her with a warm, wet washcloth.

She reached for it.

"I've got it," he said. Then he added, "Let me."

"I..."

"The correct response is 'yes, Sir'."

"Yes, Sir," she replied, the words more dutiful than agreeable. He didn't mind, as long as she did what she was told.

"Your pussy is nice and red. We should keep it that way." After washing her, then going into the bathroom to rinse the washcloth, he turned off all but one lamp before climbing into the bed. He lay next to her and pulled her close, her soft ass against his pelvis, his arm around her waist.

He needed time to unwind, but he could hold her while she rested.

"What's that against my ass?" she asked a few minutes later.

It seemed neither of them could sleep. "What do you think?"

"I'm just surprised. You can't be ready again?"

"Seems I am." He grinned. When she didn't respond, he continued, "It can wait. I can wait." No way could she be ready for more.

"You're accustomed to controlling your body's needs."

"A necessary habit, yeah." He smoothed her soft hair, realizing he liked being in bed with her. How long had it been since he'd done something like this? On some elemental level, he'd missed it.

"You lead a dangerous life."

"It can be," he agreed. "Not always." And in the times it wasn't, he trained hard, ensuring he stayed sharp mentally as well as physically. He couldn't let himself or his team down.

"So why do you do it? Why did you join? I thought you were going to college. Then all of a sudden you were gone. Without ever saying goodbye."

He adjusted her position so that she faced him and he could look at her eyes, the hazel color soft in the dimness. Even so, her face was expressive. He tracked the furrow that ran between her eyebrows. "I wanted to map my own future."

In an ironic twist, once he'd joined the military, he'd had less of an opportunity to chart the course of his life. But it had gotten him away from home, from his father's relentless control.

Long before Pierce was born, Gerard had decided Pierce was going to earn his business degree from a respected undergraduate program in the state before attending a prestigious grad school in Pennsylvania.

Gerard had expected his oldest to intern at the corporate headquarters. He'd started by franchising automotive repair shops, then moved on to ice cream parlors. By the time Pierce was in high school, Gerard had opened a few short-term, payday-type loan stores. Pierce hoped his father had moved onto something less usurious.

Enlisting in the service had been Pierce's best option to flip his family the bird.

His father had been furious at the news. He could have arranged, through his cronies, for an admission to a military academy. At least that way, the Holden name wouldn't have been tarnished. As if enlisting in the army was in any way dishonorable.

"And you stayed in because…?"

Over the years, he'd harnessed his restlessness. He'd honed himself into a lethal, precise machine. He'd been trained to think in terms of targets and situations, not about people and places. At times, Pierce wondered about the cost to his humanity.

Aware that she was still waiting for an answer, he said, "Turned out I was pretty good at it."

"I'm sure. When you focus on something, you're pretty intense."

"Do you have any complaints?"

"No." She tightened her ass cheeks. "Not a single one."

"Good."

"So no plans to get out?"

"I live in the moment." Or he had. And deployment always loomed on the horizon. "I don't look past the next mission." For the immediate future, that meant the beautiful woman in his arms.

"Any regrets?"

"About?"

"The decisions you've made?"

Not until now. "I don't deal in regrets…"

She frowned.

"But if I did, I'd regret not fucking you all night long when I had the chance."

"I'm a firm believer that we shouldn't live with regrets, Sir."

"Are you?"

With a grin, she reached for his dick. With firm, long motions, she stroked him to full hardness. "We have plenty of condoms, Sir."

"Are you sure you're not too sore?"

"Even if I was, it would be worth it."

He dropped a kiss on the top of her head.

While he grabbed a condom, she sat up against the headboard and wrapped an arm around her upturned knees. Her mussed hair flowed over her shoulders and she was watching him intently.

She looked so damn hot, and he was willing to concede that there were things he'd missed out on when he'd chosen not to pursue a relationship. "I want you on top of me," he said, "so I can play with your nipples to be sure you get off. But first, come here and put the condom on my cock like a good sub."

Ella crawled across the bed to him. She wasn't just good. She was perfect.

She took the package from him, ripped it open then placed the latex over his cockhead. "Like this, Sir?"

As she rolled it down, she squeezed and stroked his shaft, taking her time and looking up in a way that told him she knew exactly how enticing she was.

And if he weren't as disciplined as he was, no doubt he'd spill his load all over her hand.

When she was finished, he seized control again, scooping her up. She squealed, and he sat on the bed then pulled her into his lap, facing him. "There's a punishment for that intentional teasing."

"Oh? Is there?" She batted her eyelashes. "Wait. I mean, I didn't do anything on purpose, Sir."

"No? How many strokes did you give me with your hand?"

"Only as many as it took to get the condom on the right way. I wanted to ensure a good fit."

"How many strokes was it?" he asked again.

"Five? Ten, maybe."

"Last chance to be honest."

She gave a heavy sigh as she rested her palms on his shoulders. "Twenty or thirty, Sir."

"We'll go with thirty. My new favorite number for you."

That attractive little furrow buried itself between her eyebrows again. "Thirty what?"

"Strokes. I want your cunt on my dick. Stroke yourself up and down thirty times." He paused for a beat. "With your hands clasped behind your back."

Her mouth dropped open. "I'm not sure I can figure that out."

"I have confidence in you."

"So you're going to sit there and let me do all the work?"

"All of it," he affirmed.

"I thought you were a gentleman."

"Not at all," he agreed.

"So you want me to fuck you. Is that it?"

"You were pretty good with your hand. Now get on with it."

She released one shoulder and angled her body in order to reach his cock. Then she guided it toward her entrance. She was already slick, and her hot pussy wrapped around him.

"Hands behind you," he reminded her.

It took a couple of seconds for her to adjust her knees and body weight so that she could obey his order.

Slowly she began to move, first with short strokes, then longer, more confident ones as she found her balance. She flexed her hips and abs, undulating in a mind-blowing way.

Thirty? He wondered if he would survive punishing this woman.

When she was halfway through, his chest tightened. "Arch your back," he instructed, his words jagged. "I want to play with your nipples." And wanted to distract himself.

With soft moans, she continued to move against him even as she pulled back her shoulders to give him greater access.

"How many strokes so far?" The number was at least fifteen or twenty.

She responded, "Ten."

His Ella was far too clever. *Brat.*

"I need to be sure I've been taught a lesson, Sir."

There wasn't enough time to do that with her.

He gripped her nipples and tugged. Her internal muscles contracted in immediate response, which was hell on his restraint. "Keep going."

She lifted and lowered herself a dozen times before saying, "Fifteen, Sir."

Pierce gripped her hips so that he would have more control over her. He lifted her higher, then guided her all the way down. "Like that."

"Oh... Yes, Sir." She closed her eyes and tipped back her head, following his lead while he squeezed her breasts.

Her breathing became choppy, matching his own.

"Sir..."

He knew her orgasm was imminent. His wasn't far behind. "Keep going. Don't come. Next time, you might want to keep the count a little more accurately. How many are we at?"

"Twenty-nine?" Her voice held a hopeful, desperate quiver.

"We'll start from seventeen."

"Not sure that I can last to thirty, Sir."

"You can."

"I need to come."

"Fight it."

"But—"

"Count out loud." It would distract her and give him an endgame. Through his army career, he'd met numerous challenges, few more grueling than the hellish sandstorm where they'd taken a hit. He'd called on his training to get through. He could manage this.

As she continued, he realized that harsh, tough things were easier to endure than the softness of her body.

"Eighteen."

By the time she reached twenty-three, he closed his eyes to shut out the ethereal vision of her sensual response. Instead, he concentrated on the numbers she called, counting backward from seven to confuse his brain.

"Twenty-four."

Six more to go.

"Twenty-five."

Her pussy clenched him.

Five.

He breathed, but even the air smelled of her, filling his senses, making him think of sunshine. It would be something to remember during endless nights under siege.

She moaned, moving faster.

"How many, sub?" He had to remain in control, even when his grip on reality was fraying.

"Twenty-nine, Sir."

"Twenty-eight," he corrected. "Another two."

She grabbed onto him, and he opened his eyes. Her mouth was parted, her chest heaving.

He squeezed her nipples even harder.

"Now, Sir? Now, now, now?"

"Come for me, sub."

She did, in a heated rush, screaming his name, clenching then collapsing onto his shoulder.

With his eyes closed, having made certain his woman was taken care of, he set his back teeth. He gripped her hard, holding her prisoner as he pressed up inside her tight cunt.

Pierce surged and pulsed, hot cum spilling from his cock. The orgasm was every bit as powerful as the previous one.

Replete, he wrapped his arms protectively around her. "I can't get enough of you, Ella." It surprised him to realize how much he meant it.

"Me, too. I might be sore tomorrow, but it would be worth it."

He held her for a long time before helping her from his lap and onto the floor.

"I've never shared a bathroom with anyone," she admitted, crossing the threshold in front of him.

"Get used to it."

"I'm not allowed to have secrets from you, Sir?"

He met her gaze in the mirror. "When we're together, you're mine."

Her hazel eyes held a smoky look. "Yes, Sir," she acknowledged.

Possession spiked through him, something he'd never experienced with another woman.

After they'd cleaned up and returned to the bedroom, she opened a drawer to pull out a T-shirt and a pair of shorts.

"What are you doing?" he asked.

"I wear pajamas to bed."

"Not when you sleep with me."

"Naked?" she asked.

He nodded. "Naked." Then, not giving her time to voice an objection, he continued "I'll keep you warm. Now get over here."

Together they remade the bed.

She spent an unholy amount of time punching her pillow into shape.

Another person might annoy him with the routine. From her, he thought it was quirky, adorable.

Rather than making her move, he snuggled up behind her to keep his promise.

And he woke up a dozen times through the night to ensure she was warm.

* * * *

Ella rested her shoulder against the doorjamb and enjoyed the gorgeous view.

Pierce Holden—*the* Pierce Holden, her best friend's big brother and her lifelong crush—was in her kitchen, measuring coffee grounds into the filter. He was shirtless. His jeans looked baggy, so if her guess was correct, they were unsnapped.

Without her saying anything, he turned toward her.

Breath vaporized in her lungs.

"Morning," he said.

She couldn't respond.

The sight of him rendered her speechless. In the bright light, his scar was more prominent, a visible reminder of the peril he faced.

She drank him in—his muscular arms, honed abs, trim hips, lean legs. His bare feet spoke of the intimacy they'd shared and his comfort at being in her home and life.

But his eyes... He stared at her, more directly than any man ever had. Pierce wasn't looking at her—he was *seeing* her. Ever since he'd swept her onto the dance floor, he'd allowed her no secrets. He scared her, thrilled her.

When she'd awakened, alone in the bed, she hadn't known whether or not he was in the house. For a minute, she'd been convinced she was alone. A pang of grief had stabbed her until she'd shoved it away. She'd reminded herself that they had agreed to a scene, nothing more.

Then the welcome sound of running water had reassured her...until memories had rushed back. She'd recalled him putting a plug up her ass and the caning that had forced her to scream and pushed her to the boundaries of her endurance.

Then, unsure whether he'd left any marks, she'd rolled onto her side and used her fingertips to seek out bumps. That had been when she'd realized how sore her body was. She'd made a mental note to go back to her yoga classes. Barring that, a bath in Epsom salts would be nice.

She'd sat up, realizing she was nude and that she hadn't gotten cold. And that was when she'd remembered the powerful orgasms he'd given her.

The sight of his shirt and belt draped over her dresser had sent relief swimming through her, and she'd collapsed against the pillows.

If she'd experienced grief when she'd thought she was alone, how would she react when he left for good?

"You're dressed," he observed.

"Nothing more than the robe," she said. That part, she'd thought through.

Because she wasn't sure of her own emotions, and dreading the morning-after, she'd decided that being naked would leave her exposed. It was possible he'd want to put their BDSM scene behind them, maybe pretend it hadn't happened. Part of her wanted the same thing. Another more insistent part wanted it to continue. For the first time, she'd had a scene that had left her satisfied. Now that she'd experienced it, she wanted it to continue.

"Do you have any marks?"

"I think so. One or two."

"Show me."

So he wasn't just a Dom in the bedroom or for a scene. Obediently, she turned. Then, with her fingers shaking, she pulled up the robe.

"Nice."

She allowed the material to fall before facing him again. His eyes had darkened a shade, the blue turning the color of a mountain lake. "I don't think it's a good idea to permit subs to wear clothing at home."

"You don't? Subs in general? Or me in particular?"

"Everything is about you, Ella. When you're naked, it's much more difficult for you to forget that you're my submissive."

"I couldn't, regardless." How could she?

"Boundaries define relationships." He raised an eyebrow. "Evidently, I wasn't clear. Take off the robe, Ella."

With a nervous gulp, she unknotted the belt then shrugged the material from her shoulders.

"See what I mean?"

He extended a hand and she offered him the robe, which he placed on a counter.

"Any doubt about the nature of things now, sub?"

Even his words were enough to make her cunt wet. "No, Sir."

"Turn around," he said, his firm, uncompromising voice cutting, bringing her back to the moment, just as it had last night. "Spread your legs then put your palms flat on the floor."

Part of her knew it would be smarter to refuse, just have coffee and move on with her life. Every moment she spent with him brought her closer to a broken heart.

Yet his tone compelled her, urging her compliance.

Then she acknowledged the truth. It was much more than his tone that made her giddy. In spite of the risk, she wanted this and his boundaries every bit as much as he did.

She slowed her breathing and got into the position he'd said.

"You have two marks," he said, scraping his thumbnail across one.

It seared anew, and Ella wobbled.

"Wear something short to the party. I want you to remember last night."

As if she could do anything else.

"I've been thinking about how beautiful you look."

"Is that all?" she asked, unable to resist.

"And maybe laying leather across your ass." He grinned. "It's a little more personal since the belt belongs to me." He ran a couple of fingers between her legs.

It took all her self-control to remain in position.

"Fetch it for me."

He dropped his hand, and she froze.

Her motions jerky, she pushed up to a standing position. "Yes, Sir."

Before she could turn, he captured her shoulders.

She looked up at him, noting the firm set of his jaw.

"Any man who would keep another woman on the side when he could have had you is a fool. Your honesty, your transparency, the truth of your emotions is humbling. He didn't deserve you."

Though she'd told herself the same things, hearing it from someone she admired and respected was a powerful aphrodisiac.

"Now hurry. I'll add extra strokes if you stall."

She fled up the stairs, aware of him watching her.

Nudity made her uncomfortable, but there was no doubt how right he was. It did reinforce their dynamic. There was something thrilling about her seeing her lover's eyes narrow with desire when he looked at her.

After grabbing the belt, she returned to him.

He was seated on the coffee table. The sound of the coffeemaker hissing and spluttering in the kitchen added a surreal air to the atmosphere.

"This is for your pleasure," he told her.

"Pleasure?" She frowned skeptically at the leather in her hands. "Mine?"

"And something for me to remember every time I put this belt on. Over my knee."

His legs were rigid. She couldn't fill her lungs and balancing was almost impossible.

Pierce clamped one leg over hers, imprisoning her lower body. She tried to put her hands on the floor, but her fingertips only brushed it.

"Your ass was made for spanking," he said.

She tensed.

He stroked her gently.

Tension eased, despite the low-level fear churning in her.

"Perfect."

He gave her a dozen or so gentle hits and chased away the apprehension. She should have known that Pierce wouldn't give her more than she could endure.

Over time, he increased the pressure, and her body seemed to be glowing.

Everything except pleasure and being one with him fled from her brain. Her body became supple.

"Such a pretty sub," he said.

"Oh, Sir." She squirmed as arousal built. "I want…"

"Talk to me."

"Harder."

He gave it to her, not with the ferocity she expected, but a solid, steady, rhythmic beat that took her on that journey inside herself where floating and happiness combined.

She hadn't realized it had ended, but when she blinked, she was against his chest, comforted by the power of his arms.

"You've made it ridiculously difficult for me to get on a plane after tonight's party, Ella."

For the first time, she was tempted to suggest he stay. But she couldn't. Didn't dare. They had an agreement. And she was going to be strong. *Damn it.*

She composed herself, smoothing her hair and reaching for the smile she'd perfected while working at the country club.

He helped her to stand and held on to her waist.

Ella told herself to pull away, but she couldn't make her body obey her brain's orders. "The coffee sounds as if it's finished brewing."

"It does." He seemed as reluctant to let her go as she was to move.

It was as if they were both aware of how little time they had together, and how much each moment mattered.

"Cream and sugar?" she asked.

"Black."

She shuddered.

"I forced myself to learn to appreciate it. A lot of times cream and sugar are luxuries."

Another reminder of his self-discipline and the difference in their lifestyles.

Pierce followed her into the kitchen. The man consumed her, from the way her skin bore his marks to the way she inhaled his scent. He'd rearranged furniture, even made himself at home in her kitchen. Intuitively she knew it would take time for her life to become ordinary again.

He'd already placed two mugs on the counter. One was blue, glazed and had a brown moose etched on it. A friend had brought it back as a souvenir from an Alaskan cruise.

The second was one she'd bought on a whim after a bad day at work.

He read the inscription aloud, "I was supposed to be a princess. Seriously. Someone better fix this shit." He traced the gold-colored tiara. "This true?"

"Some days, I wish it were."

"Use it often?"

"No." She shook her head. Then she corrected the lie. "Well. Maybe."

"Maybe?"

"Almost every day."

Pierce filled both mugs. It had been a long time since a man had been in her kitchen. And she didn't remember one ever making her a cup of coffee. She was pretty sure it was the first step toward becoming a princess. If so, she wondered where she collected her tiara.

She added a couple of teaspoons of sugar and a dollop of French vanilla cream to her cup then closed her eyes for an appreciative sip.

When she opened her eyes, he was staring at her. "What?" she asked.

"How do you expect me to keep my hands off you when you do that?"

"Do what?" She looked up at him as she blew on the coffee.

He plucked the mug from her hand and slid it onto the counter.

Heat blazed in his blue eyes, thrilling her and making her molten.

Before she'd realized his intention, he had her back against the cold stainless steel refrigerator.

He grabbed her hands and pinned her arms above her.

Shockwaves of awareness ripped through her.

"Spread your legs, princess."

She did *not* need to be told twice. Ella opened for him.

He fished a condom from his front pocket. She wasn't quite sure how he managed — maybe through the force of his willpower alone — to open the package, lower his zipper and roll the condom down his thick cock.

"Impressive *staff*, Sergeant."

"It's amazing how resourceful I can be when something matters."

"And?"

"And fucking you right now matters more than anything."

He lowered his head toward her and devoured her mouth in a searing, sensational kiss that made her forget her own name.

"On your tiptoes, Ella."

She did as he ordered, helpless to do anything else.

Pierce pried her knees a bit farther then bent so he could position himself at her heated entrance.

"You're ready," he said unnecessarily. "Hot. Wet."

"Yes, Sir." Everything about him aroused her. "Fuck me." He must have showered while she'd still been sleeping, and she breathed in his crisp, clean scent, that of spring and seduction.

He pushed into her, impaling her, giving no quarter.

"God, yes," she moaned.

"I could hold you like this all day."

He filled her.

How long he kept her like that, she had no idea. Their gazes met. For a moment, something ghosted across his eyes. *Regret? Doubt?*

While she was still puzzling it out, he began to move. The pressure caught her unawares and she glanced away, severing the connection, the moment lost.

"The minute I get done fucking you, I start thinking about it again. I've been waiting for you to get out of bed. I'd have given you five more minutes, but that's all."

It required all her abdominal strength to take him in this position. He demanded more from her than she'd given anyone else.

It was soul-searing.

He found his rhythm in short, sensual strokes.

She leaned her head on his shoulder, realizing he was supporting her with his body weight.

He overwhelmed her.

With his free hand, he reached behind her neck and tugged on her hair.

He claimed her with another kiss, this one brutal, stealing her breath. Everything he demanded, she gave. Everything she offered, he returned. It, he, this...exceeded her dreams, and an orgasm began to unfurl deep inside. "Sir?"

"Yeah," he said, the word graveled.

Her body went rigid.

"That's it. Squeeze my cock."

She clenched her internal muscles. He rewarded her with a guttural moan, and she rode a wave of exhilaration. Big, strong, special operator Pierce Holden was weak, for her.

And then…

She splintered from the inside out.

"Fuck…" He tightened his grip on her wrists, holding her in place as he surged up, his cock becoming harder with each abbreviated thrust.

His breathing was heavy and heated against her ear. There was no place she would rather be.

She lifted her heels from the floor, leaning into him, trying to accept more from him.

"*Fuck.*" He went still for a second then groaned deep in his throat.

He tightened his hand in her hair.

She adored the way he did her, possessed her.

Her calf muscles were quivering by the time he slid from inside her. She had never been more tender than she was right then.

"I want all of you, Ella."

For her, he was like an addiction. The more she got, the more she wanted.

By slow measures, he released her hair, then her wrists.

She lowered her arms then shrugged away the tension she hadn't noticed until now. After making slow circles on skin, he rubbed her shoulders.

"I think I need a warm bath. I'm starting to fantasize about that as much as I am you."

"You've earned it. I'll make breakfast."

"You don't need to leave?" God, did that sound as desperate to him as it did her?

"I have to help my parents set up. At least that's what Morgan says. But Mom hired caterers. I suspect the command performance is more of a way for them to spend time with me." He shrugged. "I need to get in a workout and a run before I head over there. But I've got time enough for all that."

"Pancakes?" she asked hopefully. "I have a mix."

"Do you have flour? Eggs? Milk?"

"You don't need a box?"

"Just the ingredients."

"There's a cookbook in the cupboard above the stove." She pointed.

"Bacon?"

Her mouth started to water. "I like to eat a big breakfast on the weekends, but I'm too lazy to go out and get it."

"Then it will come to you."

"This can't be real. Pinch me."

"How hard? And where?" His grin made her shudder. He stepped back and she realized his jeans were still around his ankles. "You drive a man to distraction."

"No apologies for that, Sir."

"I suspected as much."

She refilled her mug then hurried upstairs to soak in the tub as he moved around, opening and closing cupboard doors and the refrigerator, clattering pans and dishes.

He didn't ask questions. And if he cursed, he did it under his breath.

Was the man competent at everything?

Within twenty minutes, he shouted that breakfast would be on the table soon.

She took her time climbing out of the bath before drying off. Then, self-consciously, she left the towel draped over a rack in the bathroom.

He was right. Being nude made her hyperaware of her submissive role.

After fluffing her hair, she pulled back her shoulders.

Then, on impulse, she went into the closet and slipped into the high heels that he liked.

When he saw her walking down the stairs, he dropped the spatula.

In that moment, she realized she had as much power over him as he did over her. She looked at the floor so that he didn't see her triumphant grin.

He'd set the table with napkins, placemats, even her nice silverware. He'd added a bottle of pure maple syrup and two glasses of orange juice.

"Pretty fancy," she noted, watching him transfer the bacon onto a platter. "I figured you would have opted for paper plates and plastic utensils."

"And I guessed a princess would appreciate a nicely set table."

"I could get used to this shit. Seriously." She moved a small pile of bacon and a huge fluffy pancake onto her plate.

He put the remaining food on his own plate.

Watching him eat was impressive. Fast and efficient.

In contrast, she wasn't halfway finished when he went into the kitchen to fetch the coffee pot to refill their cups.

He sat back to watch her.

"You're making me nervous."

"Oh?" He took a drink, unconcerned.

She swirled the last bit of pancake in syrup. "This was amazing."

"I cook when I have the chance."

"I'm surprised."

"I like good food. Don't have the temperament to go out much." He shrugged. "So I'm self-taught. Television shows, mostly."

"I pictured you as a man who watches sports or history, maybe even military. But a cooking channel?"

"I have big knives."

"Of course you do."

"And a barbecue."

"Like that old saying, men will cook if danger is involved?"

He lifted a shoulder.

Having him at the head of the table, broad and so tempting, while she wore nothing, made the meal and conversation surreal. "You know, Sir, this whole lack of clothing thing is distracting." How was she supposed to keep her hands off his inviting chest?

"If I was here longer, you'd have more of an opportunity to get used to it."

"A robe would make it easier."

"Things that are worthwhile aren't often easy."

"Is that another of your philosophies?"

"Never thought of it that way." He slid his cup onto the tabletop. "But, yeah. Like the caning you took last night. The end result was that you were proud of yourself. I thought you were spectacular."

"And I had a world-class orgasm." She popped the last bite into her mouth. "Worthwhile."

He gathered the dishes and carried them into the kitchen.

"I'll wash the dishes," she said, trailing behind him. "Since you cooked."

He nodded and folded his arms, resting his rear on the counter.

"Uhm, don't you need to get ready to go?" She rinsed the plates.

"Nope."

She opened the dishwasher and bent to pull out the bottom rack. "You're staring."

"Yes. I am."

"You're being lecherous."

"Dominant," he corrected.

"Dominant? How is gawking being a Dominant?"

"Ensuring my sub is paying attention to details."

"Lecherous," she reasserted when he ogled her ass.

"Maybe. And maybe I'm thinking of a way to fuck you this afternoon at my parents' party."

"No." She dropped the dishrag she'd been holding. "Nope. Absolutely not. Not happening."

"Want to bet?" He came up behind her, snaked an arm around her waist and brought her back against him.

Resistance vanished when he pressed his hardness into her.

Unable to stop herself, she rested her head in the seductive spot just below his shoulder.

"And do you know what else, Ella?"

"Hmm?"

"You're going to like it."

"*If* it happened, no doubt I would like it."

"By this afternoon, you'll be ripping my clothes off me."

She wiggled around, tipped back her head and met his gaze. "You're on, Sir."

He propped the pad of his thumb beneath her chin then captured her mouth in a kiss that devoured her. All of a sudden, she was no longer convinced she could resist him.

Chapter Five

"I want you to wear this one to the party." Pierce plucked a hanger with a little black dress from Ella's bedroom closet and offered it to her.

Her eyes were as wide as they were scandalized. "It's way too short. It's the kind I wear when I go out with my girlfriends. I've never even worn it to work."

"It's exactly the right length. It covers everything important."

"But…"

He perused her gorgeous body, from the fiery highlights in her hair to her painted toenails, and all the delicious, uncovered skin in between. Pierce knew he'd fantasize about this scene in future…a lovely sub, naked for her Dom. "I think it's perfect." It wasn't inappropriate in any way. Since the temperature would be in the low nineties, warm for May in the Denver area, plenty of women would be in similar dresses. "What were you planning to wear?"

She pulled out a blue, flowy thing that would cover everything, even, he imagined, her toes.

"You don't like it?"

"It's fine. For another occasion. Such as..." He searched for an appropriate word. "Winter."

Ella frowned. "It's one of my favorites."

"The other one will be easier to manage when we have mad, passionate, crazy sex."

"Would you stop?" She rolled her eyes. "We are not doing the wild thing at your parents' house."

"Have you seen the way I look at you?"

"Yes." She hesitated. "And with your military training and all, you have excellent control. So it should be easy for you to behave yourself."

"I think you've confused control with stamina." Pierce couldn't recall ever having such playful banter with a woman. He should have left an hour ago. "I could fuck you all day. But resist you? Impossible." Though he was running out of time, he had no regrets. Instead, he wished he had another hour with her. Ella was more than the perfect sub. She was a sharp, beautiful woman he enjoyed being with. There was no tension, no pretense.

He told himself it was because this was a short-term agreement. But he wished he could be sure of that. "Wear the dress. For me?"

"I'll consider it." Before he could give a fist pump, she added, "No matter what I wear, there will be no wild, crazy, passionate — whatever adjective you want to use — sex."

"Wild, crazy, passionate and *unforgettable* sex."

"I've told you —"

"It's not happening," he interrupted, repeating her words. "No way. Not ever. Uh-huh. I heard you. Every word." He grabbed the dress, tossed it onto the bed, then snagged her wrists and secured them behind her at the small of her back. Then he exerted enough pressure to force her onto her tiptoes.

"If that's true, then tell me what else I said."

"I quote... There's *absolutely* no way we are having sex at my parents' house."

"That's right, mister. I'm glad you understand, Staff Sergeant Holden. Sir. No sex at the party."

He captured her lips.

She tasted of sweetness and sass, laced with the inevitability of her surrender.

He explored her mouth, communicating in no uncertain terms how much he desired her. Pierce slipped a hand between her legs, teasing for a brief second. Then he squeezed one of her ass cheeks, hard.

She leaned into him.

"I'll see you this afternoon," he promised as he ended the kiss.

"What?"

He released her wrists then took a step back.

"Wait. You can't do that."

He grinned.

"Leaving me turned on like this is mean."

"Let's consider that stage one in my devilish seduction plan. I'm calling it Operation Fuck Ella Senseless at the Party."

"Operation...?" She gasped. "I'm warning you, Staff Sergeant Holden—"

"You'll be ripping my clothes off," he reiterated.

"I won't."

"Oh, you will. It's a promise." He traced his thumb across her bottom lip. "Do you want to start now? Get a little practice in?" The idea of Ella removing his clothing, one item at a time, made his dick hard.

She placed a hand on his chest. "Do we have time for me to take your clothes off, Sir?"

Not unless he was going to be late.

His bold submissive pulled her hand away and reached lower to grab him through his jeans.

He allowed her to, enjoying every second of her teasing. Moments before he was going to need to unzip and shove his erection into her mouth, he stopped her.

Her eyes were wide, darkened to the color of a fine, aged brandy. *Perfect.* He wanted her obsessed with thoughts of him.

"Are you stopping me, Sir?"

"Yeah."

"But you..." She licked her upper lip. "Don't you need me to take care of that problem?"

"The killer erection, you mean?" He grinned. "Nice try." Damn, he liked the fact that touching him had aroused her. This woman was his match. Now to convince her.

"If leaving me turned on is stage one, what happens next?"

"You'll find out soon."

"I'm not sure I like your tactics." She pouted, her perfectly plump lips tempting him to turn his back on his promise to his sister.

"Ella, Ella, Ella. You haven't begun to see what I have planned for you." He wanted to go caveman on her, claim her, whisk her away, lock her up, keep her naked and submissive. Make her his.

The thought made Pierce's testosterone surge.

His entire life, he'd shaken his head at friends who made decisions based on the reactions of their cocks. But now, he was a poor, miserable, besotted man, humbled like any other mere mortal.

After another kiss that left him restless, he released her. "Don't even think about playing with yourself."

"I wasn't."

"But now you are. And you're noticing how hard your nipples are, how tender your breasts feel. You might even be aware of a tingle in your clit. No doubt you're aroused, and that's made worse by the fact I won't allow you to do anything to relieve it."

"You're an ass, Sir."

"Unapologetic. Unrepentant." He kissed the top of her head. "Before I go, we need to exchange cell phone numbers." So she wouldn't have an excuse not to contact him, he programmed his information into her phone then called himself so that he could save hers.

"That's tricky."

"No need to see me out."

But she grabbed a robe, fastened the belt tight then walked outside with him.

When he looked in his rearview mirror, he saw her on the front porch, her right hand lifted in farewell. Despite their banter a minute before, her lips were pressed together, as if she was fighting back emotion. He fucking didn't like that sight. He'd rather see happiness and excitement on her features. The joy of *hello*.

When he turned at the next stop sign, he shook his head to clear it then focused on the road ahead.

Figuratively, he didn't look back. Ever since he'd been a teenager, he'd charted his course, planned the future he wanted, set goals to get there then went after them with unwavering determination.

And now, he wanted Ella.

His cell signaled an incoming message. Could be from his unit or a friend. Then he grinned. Maybe, just maybe, it was from Ella. At a traffic signal, he checked the phone.

As he should have expected, it was Morgan, reminding him to be at their parents' house at twelve hundred hours.

He replied that he wouldn't let her down then dropped his phone back on the console.

The next time he stopped, he picked up his phone again and proceeded to step two of Operation Fuck Ella Senseless at the Party — give her sexy orders.

Skip the underwear.

By the time the light turned green, there was still no response.

The woman had more reserve than he did. With a grin and to be certain he remained in her thoughts, he sent another.

Remember that I also told you to wear a butt plug.

After parking in front of his hotel, he rode the elevator to his room, where he changed into a lightweight gray Denver Broncos T-shirt and shorts before heading down to the workout room and a treadmill.

Running indoors, with the air conditioning chilling the air, was a luxury he didn't often manage. To stay sharp, he almost always chose to run outside. He had to work in heat and humidity, relentless wind, blazing sun or soul-sucking cold.

He turned off the television and set the treadmill for a brutal pace so that he wouldn't get lost in his own thoughts. Exercise that was too easy allowed his mind to wander. The more challenging the workout, the sharper his focus.

Still, images of Ella crept in around the edges of his mind. And when he inhaled, he imagined he could smell her, femininity curled around demand.

He wished for a moment that his life could be simpler, that she was the type of woman he could whisk off to North Carolina. A few of the guys he knew managed a relationship, even a marriage. But he doubted any of those women had been as adamant as Ella about not being involved with a military man.

Not that he blamed her.

He cranked up the speed, breaking a sweat, but not dislodging thoughts of her. How the hell did they even stand a chance when they'd be half a continent apart?

Even if they weren't, she wanted a life much different from the one he had to offer. He'd miss dinner most evenings.

The buzzer sounded, signaling he'd put in forty-five minutes, though it seemed like less.

He brought the speed down to a jog then a fast walk for a couple of minutes.

After his breathing and heartrate were normal, he sought out the free weights.

A woman in a halter shirt and form-fitting workout shorts sauntered in and caught his eye in the mirror. He nodded back. While he acknowledged she was beautiful with pulled-back blonde hair and a quick smile, she did nothing for him. Unlike the seductive hazel-eyed submissive he'd had up against the refrigerator a few hours ago.

No doubt. He had it for Ella Gibson. Bad. And she was worth whatever he had to go through to get her.

He finished his repetitions then re-racked his weights and heading for the stairs to take him to his third-floor room.

The knowledge that he was going to see her again soon was enough to arouse him. Even though he'd had more sex in the last sixteen hours than in the last two years, he jacked off beneath the cold spray of the shower, imagining rubbing his ejaculate all over her breasts.

Temporarily sated, he dressed in jeans and a casual polo shirt before packing his duffel bag.

His phone rang. This time it had to be Ella.

He glanced at the caller identification. His grin faded. Logan Powell.

He and Logan had been friends for years. They'd met in the service. And he didn't remember Logan calling before.

Pierce swiped the answer key. "Holden."

"Are you ready to quit playing army, yet?"

Like most men he knew, Logan didn't waste time on unnecessary pleasantries — things most people might consider manners. "What you got?"

"I'm planning to get married."

Pierce let out a long, slow whistle. "Does the woman know?"

"Well..." Logan cleared his throat.

Which meant he hadn't yet proposed. "You'd better get with it before she figures out you're an asshole."

"Knew I could count on you to be the first in line to congratulate me."

Pierce imagined his friend flipping him the bird.

"I'm going to need to expand the size of the office," Logan continued, as if the previous exchange hadn't happened.

"Ask Montrose for help. He's a logistics man." Pierce knew little, and cared even less, for administrative responsibilities. He was a tactics and assault specialist.

"We're considering combining forces. We could use a few good men."

Pierce paced to the window, thumbed aside the curtain and took a cursory glance outside. Didn't matter whether he was in Africa, the Middle East or the US. Habits were habits, and he never kept drapes or blinds open. "What do you have in mind?"

"We'll be doing some executive protection."

"I don't babysit or bodyguard." He'd trained for it. Hated it. Everything would be fine until an ambassador's wife wanted to host a tea party that would jeopardize a dozen lives, behaving as if she still lived in the Hamptons and that scones were available on any menu. "Nice talking to you. Regards to Montrose. I'll call him on my next visit."

"And we're working with friendly forces overseas."

Code for official government-sanctioned operations. American and allies. All of which would be denied if something went tits-up.

"There's some homegrown work out there, too."

Which meant counterterrorism efforts on United States soil. *Now* he was intrigued.

"The running track at the high school near your parents' house," Logan said.

"On my way." Without waiting for an answer, he hit the *end* button.

After showering, Pierce packed his duffel bag, checked out of the room then drove to the park.

Logan was already on the track, at the farthest point, running at maybe a five-mile-an-hour pace. The man must have been close by when he'd placed the call and confident that Pierce would agree to the meeting.

Before Ella, he might have told Logan to look him up in the future, another ten years or so, after he'd retired with full military benefits. But now? Couldn't hurt to listen. He could always say no.

He locked the vehicle. Since no one was close, he dropped the keys near a bush, stretched his muscles, more to be sure that he was alone than because his muscles needed it, then hit the track at a jog. Figured it would be three minutes, maybe a bit less, before Logan drew up alongside him, long enough for both of them to be sure they had no eavesdroppers.

Habits. Ingrained in both of them.

Took Logan one minute, seven seconds to fall into step. The pair could have called out a cadence to the synchronized rhythm.

Neither said a greeting.

"Resources are stretched stateside," Logan said.

Budgets and politics. Always a wicked combination. The feds didn't have the time or resources to check out every lead and perform the numerous tasks their fearless elected leaders demanded of them. And no matter who was at the top of the food chain or who was in the White House, or how much information each department said they shared, details slipped by. Connections were missed. And shit got real.

"Takes skilled people who know what they're looking for to sort through things."

During the time he'd been training to be an operator, he'd spent three days in Washington DC outwitting the FBI. Hadn't been easy. But it should have been more difficult. "Not sure why we're still talking. I don't do admin." Pierce had resisted promotions for that reason. He liked field work. He had no desire to train others. No urge to fill out more paperwork than necessary.

"We could use some team leaders. Recon."

"I'm good at stopping stuff." Barging in while others sat in a situation room and waited for updates. "But I have no patience for tedium. I think you're talking to the wrong person." No matter how tempting.

"It wouldn't be what you're used to," Logan agreed. "But you'd be on US soil."

"How often would I be home?"

"Where's home?"

Good question. Until Ella, Pierce had never considered moving back to Colorado. But now... "You have operations outside of Colorado?"

"We do. And we're working on expansion. We've been focusing on the West, California, Las Vegas. We haven't moved into North Carolina yet. Not saying we wouldn't if it mattered to you. But we would need admin, a leader. Someone to get us started."

Pierce shuddered.

Logan laughed.

"Denver area," Pierce said.

"We're looking at a lot of surveillance, gathering intel. Not the adrenaline you're accustomed to."

"You saying I may never throw another flash-bang before going in with live ammo?" Boredom was not something he thrived on.

"Yeah. Could be you'd prefer a root canal to my type of job offer."

"Heard you were shot at a few months ago."

"You sound more interested all of a sudden."

To some that made Pierce a freak. Not to Logan, he knew.

"Got a little too close. My cell phone took the worst of it."

So the position wasn't entirely without risk.

Logan named a salary range that was above Pierce's current paygrade. He'd been planning to hang around the army long enough to retire. This offer was enticing, though, and he held back a whistle.

"You'd still be serving your country."

Pierce realized Logan thought the offer wasn't good enough. That wasn't the case. In fact, Logan's figure held a comma Pierce hadn't been expecting.

Since he was overseas so much of the time, he hadn't spent a lot of money. His savings and new income level would enable him to continue his retirement plans while caring for Ella. Not in a way that Junior could, certainly. But paying the bills wouldn't be a problem. "We'll continue to talk."

Logan nodded. "Job's ready anytime." He stepped up the pace, leaving Pierce behind.

When he returned to the parking lot, there was no sign of another vehicle. After grabbing his keys and opening the door, he checked his phone.

There was no return text message from Ella.

Turned out she might be as stubborn as he was. That would make things interesting.

Time to up his game and move to step three of Operation Fuck Ella Senseless at the Party — denial.

Stroke your clit thirty times. Don't come. If you have to stop so you don't come, that's fine. But the number is thirty. No less. No more. And the correct response to my direct command is, "Yes, Sir."

He tossed the phone into the console then stuck the key in the ignition and drove to his parents' house, analyzing the conversation with Logan, thinking about Ella. Pierce arrived less than ten minutes late.

Is this still step two?

The response I'm looking for is, Yes, Sir.

He was grinning when he entered the house through the French doors in the back.

His father stood in the kitchen, a cup of coffee near his elbow. Instead of greeting his only son, Gerard checked his Yachtmaster Rolex, a watch he wore even though he was terrified of the water. "Your sister said you'd be here at noon."

"Good to see you, too, Dad." *For the first time in three years.* Pierce extended his hand.

As if he had something to prove, Gerard exerted extra pressure when they shook.

"You look well," Pierce observed. Even though the party wouldn't start for hours, Gerard was already dressed in a white shirt. A blue tie was knotted at his throat. He wore a casual blazer and chinos. And, of course, deck shoes to match his nonexistent boat.

Perhaps Gerard had just come from the office. Despite the fact it was Saturday, that was a distinct possibility. Most men opted to work from home on the weekends, but Gerard seemed to use his downtown Denver office as a refuge.

"You are planning to shower and change?"

"Not to worry. I've got extra clothes in the car. Went for a run with Logan Powell." He crossed to the coffee pot and pulled out the metal carafe to shake it. Liquid sloshed around. He didn't want any more caffeine, but grabbing a cup gave him something to do. "He's working with Joe Montrose now."

"Oh." Gerard nodded.

"Thinking about joining them."

"Does it pay better than the army?"

"A lot of things do." The fact he would still be serving his country mattered to Pierce, though. "To some people, it's not all about the money."

Gerard said nothing.

Pierce poured a cup of coffee. Even though it was tepid, it was strong.

"When you're ready to grow up and take a real job, you have a place in my business."

He took a drink, regarding his father over the rim. *Good to know nothing ever changes.* "Don't have the required degrees."

"You still have time for education. Night classes. Online. That type of thing. If getting smart matters to you, you can figure it out."

"Generous offer, Dad."

"Your mother would be pleased to have you in Colorado."

Pierce's thoughts were with one woman, and one woman only. "I haven't made any decisions yet. There's a lot to consider and work out." He took another sip, then put the cup on the limestone countertop. "What needs to be done?"

"It's time you get out of the army. Before you get seriously hurt."

As if the punctured lung hadn't been significant. "Thanks for the concern about my well-being."

"You've had a long enough rebellion, Pierce. Tell me you're ready to join the firm."

"No." Not even for a second.

His father sighed. "At some point, Pierce —"

"I will stop being a disappointment," he finished the familiar refrain.

Gerard shrugged. "Today is not that day, is it?"

He gritted his back teeth. "What does Mom need help with? Brawn can be handy."

"The caterers have most things handled."

No doubt. Laurel Holden left nothing to chance. "So why did I need to be here early?"

"I'm sure your mother will want to move some tables once she arrives home. Last- minute changes. She's worried about how everything will work when the band starts."

"Band?"

"Not a big one." Gerard shrugged. "And there'll be a small area for people to dance. But the catering company will handle the setup."

Pierce nodded.

The soft sound of a car engine rumbled in the distance, and he walked to the window then nudged aside the blinds so he could glance outside without being seen.

"Oh, for Christ's sake," Gerard snapped. "Are you going to behave as if you're in a spy thriller all afternoon?"

"Yeah. Probably."

Morgan parked their mother's sleek black sedan in the circular driveway. And Laurel remained seated until her daughter opened the door to help her out.

Dutifully, Pierce opened the front door to await his mother's grand entrance.

"Pierce! My darling, darling boy! You're home. Home at *last*." She offered a cheek.

As he bent forward to give her the air kiss, he was engulfed in a puff of gardenias and lilacs. The subtle floral blend was her signature, something she'd worn every day since he was a child.

She missed a step as she moved away, and Gerard cupped her elbow.

Pierce met Morgan's gaze. She shrugged, silently saying, yes, mimosas had been served at the nail salon.

Morgan closed the door behind them.

"Where are my babies?" Laurel demanded, facing her husband. "Didn't you pick them up?"

"Babies?"

"The dogs," Morgan supplied.

"Dogs?" Since when did his mom have more than one?

"Gerard," she wailed.

"Sorry, darling." He took her hand. "I was called into the office."

"Which means you passed the groomer's shop on your way home and left them there!" She snatched her hand back. "My God, Gerry. You're a beast." She checked her watch and shrieked. "You could have said something. Anything. They close in half an hour. We can't leave them there. Damn you. I want a divorce."

Some things never changed. His mother wanted a divorce at least once a week. Pierce believed she meant it, too. But she liked her life, her house, her status too much to change it. He couldn't recall his parents ever being anything other than tolerant of one another.

Was it any wonder he'd avoided relationships?

And his sister, too.

"Cancel the party, Morgan," Laurel said. "This time, I mean it. I'm through. I have had enough of your lack of respect, Gerry. You made a promise and didn't keep it. Again."

"We have plenty of time," Morgan soothed. "I'll go and get the dogs while you relax."

"Relax?" She pressed a ring-laden hand to her forehead. "While I'm worried about my babies and company is coming? And there are a million things to do? Gerard Holden, you *promised.*"

"I'll go with you, Morgan." Pierce fished his keys from his pocket.

After quick goodbyes, he and Morgan escaped.

"We should take the SUV," she said when he headed for his vehicle. "It's set up for the dogs."

He followed her to the garage and selected the keys from a hook. And then he saw what she meant.

The back two rows were folded down and the floor was covered with a mattress, along with numerous blankets and toys. "How many dogs are we talking about? She has one, right? Fifi."

"You should be grateful you're out of touch. She's got four of them."

"Four? Who the hell needs four dogs?" He scrubbed a hand across the top of his head. "How do you manage four dogs? Isn't that like a ton of poop? And food?"

They slid into the SUV and Morgan fastened her seatbelt without interrupting his rant. When he fell silent, she responded. "Mom's been getting a new one every year. It's her birthday present to herself. To be honest, I think she does it to annoy Dad."

"That's hard to imagine." He slid her a glance then reversed the SUV out of the garage. He maneuvered around his mother's sedan, Morgan's sports car and his own rental before turning onto the quiet two-lane road.

She gave him a general idea of where to find the groomer's shop in the historic Parker area.

"Since I've been out of touch, update me on you."

"Not much to say." She shrugged.

"Work?"

"It's good."

Could she be any more noncommittal? It occurred to him that he had lost touch, not just with his parents, but with his little sis. And at one time, he'd known everything about her, bailing her and Ella out of trouble, holding her while she sobbed over another breakup, helping her come up with an explanation for an F in algebra. "Love life?"

"Nonexistent."

"By choice?"

Morgan answered in a monotone voice, "No."

"Sorry."

"I keep busy with friends. And I'm going to a speed-dating event soon."

"Speed dating?"

"You know, you go into a room, sit down at a table with a man for a few minutes, see if anything clicks. If it does, you exchange information. If not, you move to the next table after a buzzer signals that time's up."

"Sounds intriguing."

"He said with sarcasm."

"I guess it's better than online?" he asked.

"Yeah."

They arrived at the groomer's less than five minutes before closing time. A woman with dog on a leash nodded at him. He bent to pet it, and the vicious fur ball bit him.

"Lucy is scared of strangers." The woman with hair sprayed so stiff it could have served as a battering ram in a no-knock raid, offered no apology. Instead she scooped up the still-snarling animal and walked out of the door.

"Are you okay? I am so sorry." The blushing receptionist grabbed an antiseptic wipe and offered it to him.

"It's superficial. Nothing to worry about."

"You said that when you were stabbed," Morgan said.

The receptionist's mouth dropped open. "You were stabbed?"

Sliced open was more like it. "It wasn't all that bad."

"You were in a hospital for how long?"

"More of a vacation, really." He told himself that any time he wasn't being shot at, life was easy. But it wasn't true. At times, nightmares gripped him, and he saw the cold darkness in the assailant's eyes, contrasting with the warm smile. The juxtaposition startled him so much he would awaken with a gasp.

It *had* taken a while to recuperate from the collapsed lung. The worst part hadn't been the injury. The worst part had been the fact the rest of the team was out there, doing the job while he was in a bed.

Another woman emerged from the back with four standard poodles.

"Thank you, Lisa," Morgan said, taking the leashes.

"All of those are ours?" His mouth dropped open. They were all white. They looked identical.

"Beautiful job," Morgan said.

"Bikini clip, for the summer."

"What?" Pierce asked.

"There are a number of different ways to groom them," Lisa explained. "Mrs. Holden wanted this so they'll be cool for the party. They'll grow out fast, so she can show Farrah in a couple of months. So by fall, for sure."

He shook his head. How soon until he could get back to his unit?

Each poodle had a ribbon on top of its head. And the color matched the collar, which matched a leash. "How the hell do you tell them apart?"

"Fifi, Bon Bon, Walter and Farrah all have different personalities," Morgan assured him. "Can you hold them while I pay the bill?"

He accepted the leashes as if they were a grenade.

She signed the credit card receipt.

He grimaced when he realized he'd gotten all the leashes intertwined. War was easier than dealing with this wriggling, squirming, prancing bunch of canines.

"You hold Walter, and I'll get the other three."

It would help if he knew which one that was. "Blue?" he guessed.

"Teal."

Of course.

She took the fuchsia leash from his hand, dropped it then worked it free from the tangled mess.

She continued with the pink and purple leashes until she had control of three dogs.

Lisa, failing to hide a grin, opened the door for them.

He used the key fob to open the vehicle then opened the back hatch.

"Walter goes in first."

"Why?"

"You tell me. It's an alpha thing. I figured you'd understand."

"You're right. I got it."

Walter jumped in and then turned around for Morgan to unclip his leash.

"Won't he get out?"

"They love going for rides in the car, so no."

His sister was remarkable, addressing each of the animals in a slightly different tone of voice and using finger commands to indicate what she wanted to happen.

Walter herded each of the other dogs into place as Morgan loaded them in.

"They're complicated as hell."

"Wait until Mom gets another one for her birthday."

"Are you kidding me?"

"She has a deposit on a puppy."

"Another one?" He shook his head. "I'd think one was too much damn work."

"They're highly intelligent, can work out strategy, but yeah, energetic. They have a woman who comes and gets them every day, sometimes twice if Mom is busy.

I think having a bunch of them probably isn't any more difficult than just having one."

Fifi licked his forearm then sat, looking at him with wide, bright, unblinking eyes. Her tail was the only part of her body that moved.

"It's love."

Unable to help himself, he stroked the animal behind the ear. Absently he wondered how long it had been since he'd taken time to do something like that. He was out of touch with the smaller pleasures in life, and he was no longer certain that was okay. Being sure the animals were inside, safe, Pierce closed the hatch.

He and Morgan slid into the front seats, then he started the engine and checked the rearview mirror. He saw nothing else other than electric-colored ribbons, wagging snowball tails and an endless sea of white.

He eased forward, and one of the balls of fluff stumbled sideways. "Sorry." Was he really apologizing to a dog? Maybe he should have let Morgan drive.

He turned onto Main Street, and he cringed when something warm and wet slurped up the back of his neck.

"I told you it was love."

He put up a hand for protection. It didn't work. The dog pressed her wet nose against his ear. "Make her stop."

"Aww. She loves you."

He slid Morgan a fierce scowl that made grown men take a step back.

Morgan snickered. "Just drive. They'll all settle down."

He looked at the poodle in the rearview mirror. "No licking the driver."

Fifi woofed and wagged her tail.

"I mean it."

She woofed again.

"Isn't she supposed to do what I tell her?"

"Of course." Morgan nodded. "Just like all females."

Maybe he was losing his touch. He still hadn't received his anticipated 'Yes, Sir' from Ella.

As he accelerated, the animals jostled for position and two of them pressed their noses against the windows. Fifi, however, sat behind him, chin on his shoulder. "I'm glad we brought the SUV. I had no idea. How often do you end up doing this?"

"At least once a week. I don't mind, really. The dogs are always a welcome distraction when spending time with Mom and Dad."

"What's the deal with them?"

"Neither of them are happy."

"They never have been, as long as I remember."

When they arrived home, his mother was stretched out on the upholstered chaise longue in the great room, a throw draped across her feet and a compress to the back of her neck.

Gerard was seated in a leather armchair with a notebook computer on his lap. He didn't glance up.

"My babies!" Laurel kicked off the throw.

The four dogs pranced over to her. Walter took the lead, and Fifi was last. She glanced back at Pierce with her wide, soulful eyes.

"You are all so pretty. All your ribbons are perfect. You'll be the belles of the ball. Well, except Walter. You'll be the stud." The ice pack tumbled to the floor.

Silence hung suspended.

"Aren't they adorable, Gerry?"

As Pierce could have predicted, Gerard mumbled, "Adorable."

"Gerry! Did you even look?"

He gave a half-wave to match his half-smile.

"What kind of computer is that?" Pierce asked. The sleek, titanium-looking case appeared to be both purple and blue and somewhat translucent at the same time. It had a distinctive logo on the back, part wave, part lightning bolt, all linked together. "Is that a Bonds?" Pierce walked over for a better view.

His father slammed the lid closed and placed it on the end table next to the chair. Then he covered it with a magazine about financial success. "Your mother said something about making sure the bar is set up on the patio in the correct place."

"I don't know anything about where it should go."

"Neither do I." Gerard pressed his lips together.

Laurel framed Walter's head with her hands and studied him while talking to her husband. "You know what to do. Make sure it's as close to the house as possible, at an angle so that our guests have plenty of room to walk around."

"Yes, dear."

"Morgan, be a love and fetch me a mimosa. The other one is wearing out."

"Wearing out?"

"Off. Whatever." She narrowed her eyes and waved at her daughter. "Less orange juice than the last one."

Interesting, no matter how ill she claimed to be, her lipstick was always perfect.

Pierce followed his father outside.

The bartender was already there, organizing glasses, arranging bottles of wine and beer on the top in rows, orderly enough for Pierce to appreciate. There were parts of the military that suited his personality. Precision was one of them. "Is there anything ready?"

"Yes, sir. I can get you a beer."

"Isn't it a little early?" Gerard asked

"Is it?" Not when he was expected to endure hours with his parents. If Ella were here, things would be different. Pierce turned to the bartender and gave her a big smile. "What do you have in a can?"

"I've got a pale ale from a brewery in Lyons."

"I'll try it."

The woman set it on the bar, popped it open then pulled out a glass.

"The can is fine."

Gerard shuddered. "Put it in a glass."

"Can won't get broken." He grabbed the beer then wandered over to a nearby tent.

One person was lining up chafing dishes. Another was placing three big bags of tortilla chips inside an enormous silver bowl. A third person was setting up cold packs.

He lifted the lid from one of the dishes and found it empty.

Gerard walked over to join him, a glass of something strong in hand. Whiskey, Pierce guessed.

"We have some fried chicken inside, if you can't wait until the food is served."

Pierce turned toward his father. "Breakfast was a long time ago." And he'd had plenty of exercise since then. "But I'm curious about your computer."

"Ordinary machine. Came out last year. Outdated now that the new models have been released. You can buy one yourself. There's a store in Cherry Creek. Since you won't have time before you leave again, you can order one online."

"Good to know." He leveled a stare at his father. For the first time, Pierce noticed the grooves etched next to Gerard's eyes, the ridges trenched into his forehead. "Anything you need to talk about?"

For a moment, Gerard said nothing. But he didn't snap an answer like Pierce expected.

Indecision warred in Gerard's eyes.

Perhaps for the first time ever, Pierce noticed that his father's eyes were the same shade of blue as his own. It startled him. And he wondered, with a frisson of discomfort, if they were alike in other ways as well.

Gerard opened his mouth then closed it before shaking his head. "No."

"Okay. You have my number if you change your mind." Pierce suspected both of them would be shocked if Gerard used it. "About that fried chicken?"

They walked inside. Morgan was just closing the fridge.

"Your brother's hungry." Gerard continued to the great room.

Surprise. "I can manage." Pierce opened the refrigerator door. "I don't expect you to wait on me."

"As if I would. It's in the green bowl." She picked up the champagne flute. "There's potato salad in there somewhere, too. Oh, Mom wants us to move our cars. The driveway is reserved for guests."

"I'll move them. Mom's, too?"

"Please. Hers can go in the garage."

"Where are your keys?"

"With all the others."

After glancing at the poodle-shaped wooden key hanger next to the back door, he nodded. "Consider it done."

"Thanks for being here."

"Wouldn't miss hanging out with my pain-in-the-ass sister."

She flipped him the bird behind her back as she exited the room. He grinned. She'd done that often while they were growing up, always out of sight of their parents so she could appear to be the perfect child. They were grateful to have one.

His phone dinged and he pulled it from his back pocket. Was it finally Ella?

Yes, Sir.

Air whooshed out of him. Until this moment, he hadn't realized how much the little minx had been winning the battle of wills, and how much he despised that fact.

He waited for a second message. Anything.

A minute later, he figured one wasn't coming.

Maybe he should have told her to call while she was rubbing herself. That would have been better.

Next time.

He typed in a response.

Did you do what you were supposed to?

I was about to. Sir.

Fuck. Maybe he shouldn't have asked. This morning, issuing commands had seemed like a good idea and easily accomplished. Now, though? He wasn't as sure. He'd never played with a sub who left him confounded and horny.

Text me when you're done, Ella.

Are we still on stage one?

What do you think?

I don't know. Yes? Since I'll still be needy if you don't let me come.

It's step two. Saying sexy things, including giving you orders that remind you who your Dom is.

Increasing the stakes, Staff Sergeant?

You were warned.

He prepared a plate of food for himself then took a few drinks of beer while he waited for her to respond.

Done, Sir.

His cock hardened.

You make me so damn proud. How was it?

I think I will walk funny for a while. How about letting me have an orgasm?

How about...no.

She sent back a frowning emoji. He grinned and replied with a picture of flowers and a smiling face.

Right away, as if she'd had it queued up and waiting, she replied with a red devil.

He grinned as he responded.

You're not helping your cause, princess.

She sent back an emoji that showed a smiley face that was blowing a kiss. Because he couldn't stop thinking of her, he sent one more before eating.

When will you be here?

She didn't answer right away. He hoped she was already on her way.

Pierce finished his meal then cleaned up the kitchen before grabbing all three sets of keys to move the vehicles like his mother had requested. He parked his at the farthest spot on the property, near the fence line. Far enough to be almost considered a neighboring city.

After the sedan was in the garage and the sports car outside beneath a light, he pulled out his phone. Ella still hadn't responded.

It wasn't until he was back inside that a ding signaled her message.

I don't know. An hour. Maybe two.

In other words, she was stalling, and she wasn't already on her way.

Drive safe. Let me know if you need anything.

With a frown, Pierce returned to the rental car to grab his belongings, including the garment bag he'd left hanging from the hook in the back. Avoiding his parents, he hung up all the keys then carried his beer upstairs to the guest bedroom.

As he showered, he imagined Ella in that dress, with no panties, a plug up her ass, marks on her legs — *his* marks — and her clit throbbing from her teasing.

He stroked his hard shaft a few times, but he stopped after thirty strokes, figuring he would endure the same torture he was putting her through.

Seconds later, teeth gritted against the incessant demand of his dick, he shut off the shower then vigorously dried himself with a towel.

He shaved then dressed before heading downstairs.

"What the hell?" His sister dropped a set of sketches on the kitchen counter. "I didn't know you owned a suit."

Until last week, he hadn't. "I dress up all the time."

"Uh-huh."

"Have you noticed Dad behaving strangely?"

"More so than usual?" She shook her head.

"He seems secretive about his computer."

"He was probably working and didn't want Mom to know."

"I asked if I could see it."

"It's a Bonds."

As if that explained everything.

She shrugged. "You know Dad. He's always working on something new. And he never tells anyone what he's up to."

Their mom had never complained, as long as there was money in the joint account.

Pierce fished a handful of nuts from a small glass bowl.

"Do you ever stop eating?"

"Worked out earlier."

"I should have known."

"What are you looking at?"

"Mom's thinking of adding a pool and a guesthouse with a place to change downstairs and a small apartment upstairs."

"Four thousand square feet isn't enough?" He picked up the top sheet.

"It gives her something to focus on. And maybe she hopes you'll come home more if you have a separate place to stay. I'm going to get changed."

Fifi wandered into the kitchen and leaned against him. Fortunately, she didn't get any hair, or fur, whatever it was, on him.

The doorbell rang. A cacophony of barks erupted, bouncing off walls. Sixteen paws scrabbled over the wooden floor as all four dogs dashed to the foyer.

"Traitor," he muttered as Fifi dashed away.

After putting down the drawing, he wandered toward the door in time to see his mother glide down the staircase wearing a designer dress with pumps. Her pearls were as perfect as her smile.

The bell chimed again, reverberating as if they were in a cathedral.

Gerard held out a hand toward her. "Shall we, darling?"

She pressed her fingers to the palm of his hand, and they smiled at each other as if they were a happily married couple anticipating another glorious and successful thirty years.

His father opened the door.

Game on.

Chapter Six

Ella raised her hand to ring the doorbell of the Holdens' house—more of a mansion than a home—then dropped it again to smooth her dress, pretending she wasn't shaking.

More than once she'd been tempted to text Morgan and Pierce with an apology, saying she wouldn't be in attendance. She'd rehearsed a dozen excuses, from a headache to a sprained muscle, to a forgotten commitment. But the truth was, she didn't want to see Pierce.

Even though they hadn't spent a lot of time together, she was already falling for him. That had to make her either mad or stupid. She'd had enough of military men.

What they had shared last night and this morning had been so much more than hot sex. He'd known what she needed and had given it to her. She'd had an emotional connection with him that undid her. Raw need for him made her shove rational objections into a deep dark dungeon. It was as if her inner devil had locked the door and tossed the key over her shoulder with a satisfied wink.

But every time she'd picked up the phone to make her excuses, there'd been a message from him, and her resolve had crumbled.

As she'd slid into the dress he'd selected and struggled to get the damn plug up her ass, she'd accepted that she wanted what he was offering...the teasing, the orgasms, the sensual, trusting dynamic.

And, at least for today, her desire outweighed the inevitable pain she'd experience tomorrow.

Before doubt crawled through her mind yet again, she pressed the doorbell.

Barks exploded behind the door.

Too late now.

She curled both hands into a death grip around her clutch.

Mr. and Mrs. Holden opened the door, and Walter pushed through the opening to jump up on her.

"Down!" Mrs. Holden shrieked.

Walter didn't even look at his owner.

All her tension gone, Ella scratched him behind the ears. Nothing soothed like Walter's demonstrative, unconditional love.

"He never behaves like that with anyone but you." Laurel Holden shook her head. "Be a dear and don't encourage him, Ella."

"I'm sorry, Mrs. Holden."

Laurel grabbed the dog's collar and tugged him back. "If you make me ruin my manicure, you naughty, naughty boy..."

Ella petted all the dogs, ending with Fifi—well, the one she assumed was Fifi since she patiently waited her turn.

"Come in out of the heat." Gerard allowed his wife to struggle with the animals while he held the door open farther. "You could put up the childproof gates, Laurel."

"They will go mad if we close them off from our company."

"Better them than me." He smiled big.

"Did you say something?" Laurel turned big, unblinking eyes toward him.

Gerard closed the door. "Nothing at all, dear."

"I didn't think so."

Ella looked away so the couple didn't see her grin.

"You're welcome to put your purse on the bench," Laurel said.

The bench was a stunning, custom-carved piece that dominated the entryway, built into the wall with a row of hooks above a long, thin mirror.

"There's a bar outside," the woman continued. "And we'll begin serving food in about..."

Responding to the prompt, Gerard checked his watch. "Half an hour."

"Morgan's here somewhere."

As was Pierce.

Nerves turned her stomach inside out.

Just the thought of being the focus of his attention made rational thought impossible.

The doorbell resounded once more and the dogs again exploded in frenzied barks. Ella excused herself. She placed her purse on the bench then pulled back her shoulders in a fake sign of poise.

Knowing a glass of wine would help her relax, she walked through the house toward the back door.

She thought she was prepared to see Pierce. But the sight of him, near the fireplace, made her heart stop. She paused, her gaze riveted on him.

He wore a fitted dark-gray suit with a silver tie and snowy-white shirt. Ella wouldn't have believed it was possible for him to look any more devastating than he had in denim, but he did.

His slender but muscular body was spectacular and irresistible in the tailored silk. She wondered if the suit was stage three of his plan to fuck her senseless this evening.

As if sensing her, he turned away from the man he was conversing with.

His gaze found hers.

Even across the room, his arresting blue eyes blazed with intensity. A slow smile sauntered across his mouth, and sexual heat poured through her, notching up from simmer to a slow boil.

He perused her and a slow smile slid across his face. No doubt he was wondering if she'd inserted the plug and skipped the panties as he'd instructed.

Every noise in the room amplified in her ears as her nerves slammed into hyperawareness, fueling her need to escape.

Knowing he'd seek her out soon, she exited through the French doors onto the patio.

The temperature already hovered near ninety degrees, and numerous large, colorful umbrellas had been opened.

She ordered a glass of chardonnay from the bartender then headed toward the water feature that Mrs. Holden had installed last year, a stunning waterfall and pond. An aspen tree provided some shade, and she took a fortifying sip of the wine.

"So. Did you go home with him?"

At the sound of Morgan's voice, Ella spun. "What?" She glanced around the Holdens' patio, hoping none of the anniversary party guests had overheard her friend and praying that no one knew she and Pierce had spent the night together.

Morgan clamped her arm on Ella's elbow and dragged her closer to the waterfall for privacy. A small brown sparrow that had been splashing on top of a rock shook its wings then took flight.

"Details." Morgan kept her grip tight, as if afraid Ella would try to run away. "All of them."

"About...?"

"What happened last night after I left the bar?"

Ella's pulse picked up as she scrambled to find an answer that would appease her friend.

"You know what I'm talking about." Morgan rolled her eyes. "Randall."

Randall. So Pierce hadn't said anything. In relief, Ella exhaled. "There are none. I didn't go home with him."

"Thank God. I was worried about you. He gives me the heebies." Morgan shuddered with exaggerated movements.

Ella grinned. Though she hadn't been captivated with him, she'd been looking at him through a realistic lens, inventorying faults as well as strong points, trying to ascertain whether he was a man she would want to date and perhaps spend her life with. He might have been egocentric, but so were a lot of men she interacted with at the country club. It didn't mean they were bad guys. "What don't you like about him?"

"He didn't honor a sub's safe word at a BDSM play party."

The voice, masculine, calm, familiar, made desire arrow through her.

Pasting on a false smile, the one she wore almost all day, every day during the work week, she turned to face Pierce. She inhaled his crisp scent and memories crashed through her. Bravado fled, and her knees threatened to buckle.

"Ignore my big brother," Morgan apologized. "He says inappropriate things."

If Morgan had any idea…

"Ella." He extended a hand.

Having no choice, unless she wanted to make Morgan suspicious, Ella shook his hand. He held hers for too long, squeezed, but not too hard, just a reminder of how well he knew her and what they'd shared.

"I'm glad you could be here."

Since he didn't let her go, she tugged away from his grip. "I wouldn't have missed it." The lie fell from her mouth. Her voice hadn't wavered and betrayed her inner emotions.

"Is that true about Randall?" Morgan asked him. "I've heard things about him from some of my friends, but that's not one of them."

"It happened."

"Ick." Then Morgan propped her hands on her hips "Wait." With a fierce scowl, she demanded, "How do you know it's not just a rumor?"

"I was there."

"What?" Morgan screeched. "What were you doing at a BDSM club, anyway? And Randall is a Dom?"

"No. He's a fake. That makes him a menace."

"Hold on a minute." She narrowed her eyes. "Which club are we talking about? One in Denver?"

"None of your business, little sis."

"I need details, Pierce. And I mean it."

"What do you know about BDSM clubs?" He raised his eyebrows.

Ella took a drink of wine to hide her smirk.

"Mom's waving at you."

"Again?" Morgan sighed, glancing toward the tent where Laurel was standing next to the caterer.

"I think she wants another mimosa. Or something."

"Oh. God. I'll be right back."

"That was mean." Ella frowned at Pierce when Morgan strode off, steps certain over the uneven flagstone surface. "Your mom wasn't even looking this direction."

The smile on his face was unrepentant. "She's going to need something sooner or later."

"Still —"

"I wanted to be alone with you." He took a step toward her, crowding her space.

Tension unfurled in her, triggering the fight or flight instinct. She did neither. Instead, she froze.

Everything about this man fascinated her.

While she'd been at home, she'd told herself she could, would, resist him. But when he stood scant inches away, and they breathed the same air, her intention was crushed.

"I've been looking forward to seeing you again since I left your house."

"Planning your strategy is more like it." She kept her words light, hoping to wedge some emotional distance between them.

"Yeah." He raised one shoulder. "It might be time to move into stage three of Operation Fuck Ella Senseless at the Party."

"Wait." She pretended to be a woman in control, someone accustomed to this kind of raunchy flirtation. "What was stage two?"

"Saying sexy things. Reminding you who your Dom is."

"Do you behave this way with all the women you pursue?"

"I don't pursue women. Or I didn't…until you."

"Are you saying—?"

"That you're different? That I'm different when I'm with you? That I've never experienced anything like this before?"

She waited.

"Yeah. All of those things."

Ella couldn't breathe. This man. Every word was well chosen and perfect, further eroding her resistance to him.

"You look beautiful, Ella. As I knew you would."

When he spoke, he studied her, sealing the connection of their gazes, as if there were no other person on the planet who interested him.

"The dress…"

He'd made an excellent choice, she had to admit. It flowed nicely, but it was fitted enough that the gentle breeze didn't lift it.

Before she'd left the house, she'd raised the hem and looked in the mirror. It had taken some contortions to see over her shoulder and angle her head so she could ascertain whether he'd left a stripe on her skin. He had. One.

"And did you wear panties?"

Stage two, say sexy things. Even though she knew what he was doing, the strategy still worked. Her pulse became thready. Ella knew she'd reacted as he'd intended. "I skipped them."

He sucked in a breath. "And the plug?"

Distracting her, Walter dashed through the open French doors and headed toward her. He angled his tall, strong body between her and Pierce, as if trying to protect her. "Hello, Walter. Have you come to say hello again?"

She swore he gave her a doggy grin. Walter plonked himself down, one of his legs on her foot, as if he were a prince and had every right to sit wherever he liked. Ella placed her glass on one of the waterfall's rocks and scratched him behind an ear. "I think he's protecting me."

"It will take more than a dog to keep me away from you." Pierce's smile was feral. She shivered. "About the plug, Ella...did you follow my order?"

She took a breath. When he used that tone — command, wrapped in a sensual huskiness — she was undone. "I did."

"Yes?"

"Yes, Sir," she amended. As she said the words, something inside her shifted. Her voice became softer. She wanted to please, to surrender. Her reaction to him was as much physical as it was emotional.

She met his gaze. The approval and longing there made her glad she hadn't disappointed him. "I inserted the plug." Another in a long line of firsts for her with this man. Being both bare and stuffed for him was exhilarating. The way he pushed her past her inhibitions was liberating. And each time she did something new, it undermined her determination not to fall for him. Then she shocked herself by adding, "And I re-waxed my pussy, as well, Sir."

"Fuck." He uncapped a water bottle and took a long drink.

"Maybe you shouldn't have asked, Staff Sergeant?" *Stage two, Sir. Say sexy things.* She just had no idea how difficult it was to be bold this way. Teasing him turned her on.

"You're playing a dangerous game."

"Am I?" Maybe she was. Since they had such a short time together, it was worth it.

"You already know I intend to fuck you."

"And I've already said not that's not going to happen." She picked up her wine, and Walter nuzzled her free hand.

When Pierce spoke, his tone vibrated with a deep, soft rasp. "Did you stroke your clit?"

When she'd first read the text, she'd thought her phone might start to sizzle from the heat of his words. "I did. Sir."

"And?"

"It aroused me." He had to know that. "But not as much as the way you kissed me and played with me before you left my house this morning."

"How turned on are you right now?"

Ella tightened her grip on the glass.

"Scale of one to ten. One being tepid."

"And ten…?"

"Ready to come the second I slide my finger between your legs."

She shouldn't have asked.

"Eight?" he guessed. "Nine."

Nine and a half. "Five or six."

His lips quirked. No doubt, he recognized she was lying. "Shall we see, princess?"

"No!"

Walter jumped to his paws.

Scandalized, she glanced around the patio and exhaled when she realized no one was close enough to hear.

She petted Walter to soothe him. But Pierce's smile was broader than ever. Damn him.

"So what's the real answer, Ella?"

"Nine."

"Meaning it would take me a minute or two to get you aroused?"

She closed her eyes. "Closer to a ten."

"It's a ten for me."

"What?"

"I thought of you in the shower."

"Did you…?"

He waited.

"I mean…"

"Ask."

Walter sat again, and she angled her chin. "Did you jack off?"

"Yeah. But I didn't come. I fantasized about you, about seeing the mark I hope is on your skin, about the thought of you playing with yourself, about giving you everything you want."

One more time before he left. So tempting. So wrong.

Mr. and Mrs. Holden emerged from the house and stood near the food tent. Walter seemed to forget about Ella and dashed over to his owners. The other dogs gathered around him and jockeyed for position.

Morgan, composed and gorgeous, stood in front of the dogs, got their attention and signaled for them to sit.

As if choreographed, they all plonked down at the same time, looking regal and impressive.

After giving another hand signal, Morgan walked off to one side. A few people snapped cell phone pictures, and she wished she'd held onto her purse.

Mrs. Holden waved a hand, and her numerous rings winked in the overhead sun. "Thank you for coming to help us celebrate our thirtieth anniversary."

The crowd clapped, and a few whistles split the air, making Bon Bon tip her head.

Pierce moved into place beside Ella, as if they were a real couple. She liked having him next to her so much that it terrified her

"Please help yourselves to food," Mr. Holden said. "Later, we'll have cake, a champagne toast, and a band."

The caterers pulled back the siding on the tent, removed lids and cellophane then left the area.

"Shall we?" Pierce extended a hand toward the tent.

Nothing could have surprised her more. "You need to interact with other guests."

"I will do that later. For now, I like watching you, imagining the plug in you."

While embarrassment gnawed at her, he grinned then picked up his water bottle as if he hadn't said something scandalous.

She gulped down the rest of her wine before handing the empty glass to one of the servers.

In the buffet line, he introduced her to several of his parents' friends, and as they walked toward a table, he rested his fingers at the small of her back. He'd done it at the bar, as well. She found it protective and possessive as well as endearing.

He guided her toward a table with a few empty seats. "Is this okay?" He pulled back a chair for her.

"You don't have to sit with me, Pierce."

He scowled. "Of course I do. I take care of my woman."

She appreciated seeing this side of him, interested in others and asking thoughtful questions, all while glancing over at her on numerous occasions and being sure to include her in the conversation.

When asked what his job was, he kept his answer vague, making it sound as if he spent his days buried in administrative responsibilities.

"Watch out for those paper cuts, Holden," one man said. He laughed at his own joke.

"Keep a first-aid kit in your desk drawer," another added.

Pierce took a drink of water then leaned forward to ask the person across from him how business was.

Not long after dinner, some people, especially those with kids, began to leave.

The catering crew removed some tables and rearranged others. At the same time that the band was setting up, two men brought in big panels that resembled wood but seemed thin and somewhat flexible. They laid them over the flagstones and taped the seams together to create a dance floor.

"You don't mind that teasing?" she asked him later, after the Holdens had sliced their cake and champagne had been shared.

He shook his head. "They don't matter in my life any more than they did ten years ago. You, on the other hand..."

The band started, playing a slow, easy-listening song made popular by Otis Redding decades ago.

"Dance with me."

Tonight, it was an invitation rather than the order it had been at the honky-tonk. "I can't believe you want to dance."

"I don't. But I want you in my arms, and I figure it's the only way you will let me put my hand on your ass."

She grinned.

"Is that true?"

From beneath her lashes, she looked at him. "It could be."

He stood then offered his hand, followed by his irresistible grin.

Instead of leading her in the direction of the makeshift dance floor, he surprised her by guiding her toward the privacy of the waterfall...which, she told herself, she should have expected.

Overhead, the sky was pink and orange, with beautiful swirling clouds, as the sun set behind the Rocky Mountains. The temperature had dropped a couple of degrees, so she didn't object when Pierce held her close.

As he had last night, he led, but not in a dance step that she knew. This was more of an intimate sway. Without being told, she responded, lifting onto her tiptoes to lean into him and wrap her arms around his neck.

"Perfect." He pressed one palm to the center of her back with his fingers splayed. Then he moved the other to her bottom. "I could keep you here forever."

A lump lodged in her throat. There was nothing she wanted more. The impossibility of it made her heart hurt.

The instinct for self-preservation urged her to pull away. But the yearning to be with him won. Ella reminded herself that once he left, she would hurt anyway. Might as well make it worthwhile.

They moved together, as if they were in a private, magical world created for the two of them.

"You've gotten to me, Ella. Being here with you instead of alone somewhere is torture."

"Good."

"You've got an evil streak." The words, said into her ear, sent a shiver skipping down her spine.

In exaggerated shock, she asked, "Do you want me, Staff Sergeant?"

"Is it obvious?"

"You left me wanting earlier." And the need had continued all day.

"I've warned you about your dangerous game."

She smiled, enjoying the banter.

For the first time in her life, she rested her head on a man's shoulder, knowing she was safe, protected. For now, she wanted to savor the moment.

All too soon the music faded. They swayed to a stop several seconds later, when others were returning to their tables.

He tucked her hand inside his as he led her back to their chairs. She'd never been with a man as attentive as he was.

As he had earlier, he pulled back her chair. "Would you like another glass of wine?"

"No." She shook her head. "I need to drive home."

"Holden, there you are!" A tall, thin man with a receding hairline rushed over and stuck out his hand.

Pierce stood. "Harold Loughton? Haven't seen you in years."

"Since I was in high school."

The two shook hands.

"What the hell are you up to? I know your dad wants you to join the firm."

"May I introduce you to Ella Gibson? She's a longtime friend of Morgan's and mine. Ella, Harold Loughton. His father was in business with my dad. Harold went to work for the company after he graduated from college, if I remember?"

"Yep, yep. You're absolutely right." Harold nodded. "Good to meet you, Ella."

The man grasped her hand and squeezed with far too much enthusiasm. She extracted herself from his grip without responding to his greeting.

"Mind if I join you?" Without waiting for an answer, he grabbed a chair, turned it backward then sat. Harold bounced his right leg, radiating perpetual-motion energy. "You still at Fort Bragg?"

"Yes." Pierce uncapped his water and took a drink. She watched the way he looked at Harold. Cautious, questioning, distant.

"Aren't you bored out of your mind? Ready for some real work? You know, you could make a difference in the world. I'm still working for your dad's company. VP of Accounting. But I don't go around bragging."

"No?"

"Trying to keep all the money straight. He's expanding again. Enough work to keep an army busy. Get it? Keep an army busy. And you're an army guy!"

She wondered if the man ever took a breath.

"We could use someone to train store managers. I'm betting you've been taught some leadership skills. At least that's what some of the veterans we've hired say about the service. Platoons and units and all that."

"All that," Pierce echoed, sounding as if he were in agreement.

"Hey, I'm serious, man. We could use some brains at headquarters."

Since Harold seemed to be settling in for a long visit, she excused herself.

Pierce stood and squeezed her hand. "I'll find you."

"Don't worry about me."

"I'll find you."

Since arguing with him would serve no purpose, she nodded. "It was nice to meet you, Harold."

He lifted a hand in acknowledgment but continued talking to Pierce.

She visited with a few people as she made her way across the patio. Since Morgan was occupied, Ella decided it was a strategic time to leave. Better than saying goodbye to Pierce. *That,* she wasn't sure she had the strength to do.

After looking over her shoulder to confirm he was still talking with Harold, she found Mrs. Holden. Since the dogs were gathered around their besotted owner, Ella petted them all, giving Walter a little extra attention. He angled his head to make it easier for her to scratch behind his ear. Smart boy. "Thanks for inviting me. I had a wonderful time. The food was great. The band is fabulous. You throw the absolute best parties."

"I'm glad you could make it." Mrs. Holden pulled her shoulders back, preening at the effects of the compliments. "You'll have to join Morgan and me for mani-pedis some Saturday morning. They serve mimosas."

"I'd enjoy that." Before heading inside to collect her purse, she added, "Happy anniversary."

Ella's hand was curved around the front door knob when Morgan caught up to her. "Wait! Don't you even think of walking out of here without talking to me!"

She dropped her hand and turned to face her friend. "That was a great party, Morgan. Everything was perfect."

Morgan narrowed her eyebrows. "Did I see you dancing with my brother?"

"Yeah." She might as well admit it so Morgan would leave her alone. "It was a pity dance. He saw me standing there alone with only Walter for company." It hadn't happened in quite that order, but she didn't mind playing loose with the facts.

"That didn't look like a pity dance to me."

"I haven't got a clue what you're talking about."

"I know what I saw."

"You saw your brother being polite."

She cleared her throat. "As if. The words Pierce and polite don't belong in the same sentence. I'm telling you, this conversation isn't over. I want answers."

"There's nothing to tell. You need to get back to your guests."

Morgan's scowl grew fiercer, more determined.

"Go." *So I can get out of here before Pierce notices I'm gone.*

"I'm telling you…"

"You already made that threat. You need a new one." Ella grinned and hugged her friend. "Give me a call."

"Don't think I won't."

"Not ever," Ella promised. She fished her keys from her clutch then left the house, closing the door behind her with a decisive click.

She paused on the porch to draw in a breath. Then, before Pierce could come after her, she walked toward her car. Since so many people had already left, her car was isolated in the distance. The outdoor lighting was faint as she moved away from the house and no moon brightened the sky.

When she neared her car, she pushed a button to unlock it and turn on the interior lights.

She froze. Pierce stood next to the driver's door, arms folded, his expression unreadable in the dimness. She sucked in a short, uneasy breath.

"Did you think you could escape without me noticing?"

"I hoped," she admitted.

"Because…?"

"Please, Pierce. I can't do this."

"Do what? Leave without letting me kiss you goodnight?"

She took a shallow breath. "You're dangerous."

"What harm can there be in one kiss?"

The question hovered on the night air. Because she knew the answer, she remained silent.

"Come here."

Yes. In the end, it wasn't a battle. She dropped her keys into her purse then went to him. And now that she was so close, she could read him better, saw the set of his jaw and the hurt in his eyes. *Hurt?* How was that possible? She'd expected frustration, maybe even anger. But the raw flash of honest emotion made her wonder if this might be more than a simple weekend affair for him.

"Damn it. It's impossible for me to think of anything else when you're around."

The car's interior light faded, and the darkness seeped around them, leaving them shrouded in privacy.

Pierce put his hands on her shoulders and guided her around so that her back was to the car, using his body to shield hers. No casual passerby would see who he was with.

"A gentleman to the end."

"You're my woman."

As if that says it all.

He feathered his fingers into her hair and pulled back her head. Then he nudged a knee between her legs. "Open your mouth."

She surrendered...because she wanted to more than she wanted to hold on to her sanity.

Pierce touched her tongue with his own, in a seductive dance, and he tightened his grip. She was aware of the band still playing in the far-off distance, an upbeat song that electrified the night.

The kiss—his kiss—was hard and deep, devouring her, communicating the words he hadn't said, the promises he wanted to make but never would. It wasn't enough for her.

Ella returned his kiss and opened her mouth wider. She lowered herself so that her pelvis was a fraction of an inch above his thigh. He put his hand on her back for support.

The touch of her bare pussy to the rough material covering his muscled leg almost made her come. She groaned. She knew he had a plan to seduce her and was so confident of it that he'd told her all the stages. He'd aroused her, said sexy things, reminded her she was submissive. No doubt he had moved onto the third step, and so far, it was working.

Without shame, she rubbed herself against him.

He murmured something indistinct, but she recognized it as encouragement. She rocked her hips forward and her labia parted, exposing her clit. The plug shifted deeper, filling her more.

Pierce ended the kiss, leaving her mouth swollen, her lips parted. He pulled her hair harder, forcing her to arch her back. She gasped and shifted her position.

"That's it. Rub yourself on me."

Operation Fuck Ella Senseless at the Party... Heightening her arousal was part of his strategy, but it didn't matter. Need sucked rational thought from her brain.

He slid his hand beneath her dress and his palm warmed her flesh. She tried to say his name, but nothing more than a moan emerged.

He rained kisses down the column of her throat and ended at the tiny indentation at the hollow.

"Do it thirty times."

"I can't." *Shouldn't.* She would be begging him to fuck her soon and ripping off his clothes as he'd promised.

"You can." He held her in position. "It would be better if I fingered your hot cunt at the same time."

"Then do it."

He hissed, and Ella gave herself a mental fist bump. Getting that reaction from Staff Sergeant Pierce Holden was no easy feat.

He offered a finger and she sucked, pantomiming giving him a blow job.

"That will be quite enough."

When she didn't stop, he captured her chin.

"How far would you like to take this?"

A ridiculous, reckless part of her wanted to push it until she achieved the reaction she wanted. *Which was...?* A spanking? A fucking? Making it as difficult for him to forget her as it was going to be for her to forget him?

She sucked his finger deeper into her mouth.

"Oh, Ella." He exerted a small amount of pressure on her cheeks, and she was forced to release him.

He slid his hand between her legs.

"You may want to get busy. I told you to rub yourself thirty times. I meant it."

"Yes, Sir." She had to adjust her balance. And he jostled his leg, throwing her forward. Her breath whooshed out and she let out a loud *oomph.*

"One," he prompted.

She recovered her breath and he inserted a second finger. The sensation, with their hands bumping and the plug moving, overwhelmed her. Still, she sought more.

"Delicious sub."

Lost in their sensual, naughty, risk-taking play, Ella lost count of the times she'd stroked her clit.

He still had a hand in her hair, keeping her arched.

This image would fuel her fantasies for months.

Stunning her then, he added a third finger, splitting her apart. There was no way she could do this…

She struggled for breath.

"How aroused are you now?"

Dazed. This time she told the truth. "Nine point nine."

"That pleases me."

"Oh, Sir!"

"Now stop."

"What?" She blinked. "You can't mean that." *Again.*

One at a time, he eased his fingers from her and also loosened his grip on her hair. "It's your choice. We can leave it as is, and I can wish you a good night."

She waited. "Or?"

"We can finish it, and you can rip my clothes off in one of our vehicles. If you prefer, we can go back to your house."

"You have a plane to catch." Ella couldn't endure him walking out of her house a second time.

"It's a red-eye. I've got a couple of hours."

Holy fuck, she was so turned on, she was going to lose it if she didn't come. She could always say no, but the release he gave her was so different — *better* — than any orgasm she'd ever given herself.

All day, since he'd left her unfulfilled at home that morning, he'd created tension in her. He'd ratcheted it up with each calculated message he'd sent and the fact he'd made her stroke herself just to the point of orgasm before she'd left for the party.

But the truth was, being in his arms near the waterfall, with her head on his shoulder, had been enough, all by itself, to melt her resistance to him. "Where is your car?" It was larger than hers, making it more appealing.

"Over there." He pointed to a place even more secluded, beneath some tall pine trees.

"I think yours is a better choice."

He nodded.

"Give me a second. I want to get in my car."

He stepped to one side, and she opened the door to slip her purse beneath the driver's seat. Then she grabbed a package of sanitary wipes from the center console. "I think we may need these." She opened the foil package and pulled one out.

"Good call." He wiped his hands then snagged her wrist.

"Wait!"

Instead of doing as she said, he reached over her to flick the door closed.

"You read my mind, Staff Sergeant."

"As usual."

"So, if you are reading my mind..." Ella trailed off.

"You're planning to start by unknotting my tie and opening a few buttons, even though most women would choose to remove my jacket first. A few would even fold it or hang it from the hook in the back. But since you're as impatient as I am, you'll pull my shirttails out of my waistband without thinking about my jacket. Then when you do, you'll be hoping I manage it myself since you'll be busy working on getting my cock out and sucking it deep into your throat."

"Oh, God..."

"Is this still step two?"

"Either that or my keen imagination. Come on."

More than any man she'd been with, he made things fun.

With customary impatience, he led her to his vehicle. He, too, used his remote to open the locks, and she saw him scanning the surroundings, taking them in, looking for risk, ensuring her safety and modesty.

He opened the back door and tipped his hand sideways, indicating she should enter.

She slid across the soft leather seat, all the way to the far side.

Pierce took another look around, including a long surveillance of the main house and yard, then nodded. Once he was inside the car, he pushed the button to lock the doors.

He didn't advance on her until the light faded, but then...

He grabbed her waist and pulled her over to him. She yelped from the surprise, and he silenced the sound by yanking her over his lap. He bounced his right knee a couple of times, tipping her off balance, her ass in the air.

He flicked her dress aside. "Stay still."

When she didn't, he gave her a solid smack on the rear, driving the plug deeper.

The sound reverberated in the car and her ears. It satisfied, soothed and settled her.

"Follow orders. And when in doubt, 'yes, Sir' is always a good response. Didn't take you long to forget."

"Maybe I need constant instruction." She couldn't believe she'd said that. Why couldn't she resist goading him?

He reached into his jacket pocket. She realized he'd pulled out his cell phone. He turned on the flashlight app and looked at her naked bottom. A moment later, he groaned. "You do have a mark."

"And the plug. I think I told you that, Sir."

"Yeah." Using his free hand, he slid a couple of fingers in and out of her damp pussy.

She stilled. Maybe if he didn't have any idea how close she was, he would continue until she came...

Instead, he turned off the flashlight and dropped the phone back into his pocket then slipped his fingers out of her cunt. "Sir!"

He helped her up and guided her into place, straddling him. "What do you want?"

"You. Inside me. I think you've given me blue balls."

He laughed. "That happens to men."

"It means a person is in pain from the blood flow from not being allowed to come, right?"

"More or less. But if we're being technical, the term refers to what happens when the testicles —"

"So blue clit. Whatever. Call it what you want. Just get me off, now. Please."

Even in the darkened interior of the car, she knew he'd drawn his eyebrows together.

Taking the initiative, she shifted her weight. His legs were spread so that her swollen clit was elevated and exposed. "You were right."

"About?"

"The way I'm going to undress you." She tugged on the knot in his tie, loosening it. Then, patience gone, she lifted his collar so she could yank the tie up and over his head. She dropped the material, still knotted, to the floorboard before she began work on his buttons.

When the top three were undone, she sucked in another breath. She ran her fingertips across his chest, and the feel of his honed muscles sent shockwaves through her. "I want you."

"Not even half as much as I want you."

"This has to come off." She slid her palms beneath the lapels of his jacket. Always helpful, he leaned forward. "Good. Now shrug."

"You're bossy."

"Bluc balls, Sir," she countered.

"We'd better take care of that."

"Yes, please."

He helped her with the jacket. She tossed it on top of the tie.

Losing all sense of control, she grabbed handfuls of his shirt and yanked it free from his trousers.

Her pussy throbbed with incessant need.

The sounds of their frantic breaths filled the car's interior.

She fumbled with the last few buttons, and he brushed her hands aside and opened the next one down. Since he was busy, she got to work on his belt buckle. In the dark, with desperation driving her, she kept losing her grip.

Finally, once she had it open and pulled through the loops on his trousers, she unfastened his waistband then dragged his zipper down.

He'd worn no underwear.

"That is so freaking hot, Sir." She took hold of his hard cock and stroked it. His balls were already tight. "You're as ready as I am."

"Have been for hours."

"Oh, my God. Condom? Tell me you have a condom."

"In my wallet." His fished it out of his back pocket, and since he'd lifted his hips, she took the opportunity to work his slacks down to his knees.

While he opened the wrapper, she returned to stroking his shaft. She became wetter just from touching him. "Fuck me, Sir."

"I think Operation—"

"You win. Now do me. Do me. Do me. *Do me.*"

"Are you asking for something, sub?" Even though he'd tried for serious, laughter lurked behind his words.

"Yes, please. Your beautiful dick, Sir."

"Where do you want it?"

"In my hot cu —" Before she could finish the word, he moved her from his lap and onto the seat beside him.

Then he slid a palm beneath her buttocks and scooted her a few more inches. "I want to be on top of you."

She grabbed the bottom of her dress and started to pull it up, but he stopped her.

"Leave it. If anyone comes, I want you covered." He loomed over her.

Since her vision had adjusted to the dark she could make out the ferocity in his eyes. She dropped the material.

"The next time I see you, I may cut your clothes off you." He pressed her down as he slid his cock into her.

"Sir." She sighed.

"Rub your clit."

It took some effort to work her hand between them, and she gasped when her nail abraded the swollen flesh. She'd never played with herself when having sex before, and a thrill zipped straight through her. Between that and the plug, she was about undone. "Please tell me you won't make me stop at thirty."

"Keep going." He surged into her.

Pierce overwhelmed her. His gorgeous face dominated her vision, and she breathed in his clean, musky scent. "So, so, close, Sir."

"Come when you're ready, Ella."

Unsure whether her clitoris could endure any further torment, she pulled away her hand and surrendered to the dominance of his cock.

She wrapped her arms around his neck. Then she squeezed her eyes closed as the orgasm rocked her. Ella cried out his name, and he swallowed it with a sensual kiss at odds with the way he fucked and the force of her climax.

Everything he did created dissonance, intensifying her reactions. Her brain couldn't figure out what he was doing before he'd moved on to something else.

When she opened her eyes, she saw his were closed and his head was tipped back. She loved seeing him this vulnerable. It made her heart swell with love... Ella shook her head to force away the thought.

Pierce shortened his strokes, and she responded by tightening her pussy around him. He moaned deep in his throat. A frisson of satisfaction raced through her. She loved knowing she had some power over him.

The first spurt of his ejaculate caused his body to go rigid, and she tightened her grip on him.

"Damn," he said a long time later after dropping a kiss on her forehead. "I love being inside you."

His arms were shaking, and she realized that he'd held his body away from hers the entire time they'd been having sex. He had made certain he didn't crush her, even while she had been pulling down on his neck.

"I haven't done this in a dozen years. Wait. Make that more than a dozen years."

"It's a first for me."

"I popped your backseat cherry?"

She giggled as if she were a schoolgirl. "That's one way to put it."

"I'm honored. Proud."

"Gonna notch your bedpost?"

"Wouldn't be worth it." Where his voice had been gentle and teasing, it became serious. "You're the only woman who's ever mattered."

Ella wasn't quite sure how he managed it, but one moment she was beneath him, the next she was on top. It took her a second to figure out what had happened. "Do you have superhuman strength?"

"And reflexes." He pumped his arm.

"Of course. And reflexes."

"Always good for you to show proper appreciation for your lover." He studied her. "And Dom."

Her smile faded as reality plowed into her, dragging her under a wave of emotional devastation. He was neither. Could never be.

"Ella?" He frowned and tucked her hair behind her ear. "You okay?"

All lightness fled. "That was pretty intense." She meant more than the sex. Her words were honest, more honest than he might have realized.

He disposed of the condom in a napkin that had been in the glovebox.

She smoothed her dress into place, pretending everything was fine, that she wouldn't wake up tomorrow with her heart in a thousand jagged pieces.

He buttoned his shirt while she ran her fingers through her hair, trying to tame the wild mess. "Sure you don't want to move to North Carolina?"

For a second, her mind raced. Her heart wanted to seize the opportunity. "It's not the place that's the problem." Being by herself while her man was gone fifty percent of the time was.

"You're wounding my ego."

"Flex your muscles when you look in the mirror. That will help."

"No doubt."

Something threaded through his voice, as well. Tension? Was he trying to be as light as she was? As disingenuous?

To occupy herself, she picked up his jacket and tie and placed them on the seat next to her, then reached for the door handle.

"You don't want to talk for a bit?"

"People will have noticed you're gone. We don't want questions. And... I need to get home. I didn't get much sleep last night."

"Wait there."

He exited the rental then came around to her side to open it and offer his hand. Once the interior light was illuminated, she noticed he'd missed fastening a button. Unable to help herself, she fixed it.

"Thank you."

"You'll want to tuck your shirt in, Staff Sergeant."

"Is it okay if I leave the lipstick on my face?"

He kept hold of her until they arrived at her car.

She faced him, her buttocks on the car front fender. He took a step toward her and placed his feet on the outside of hers, trapping her.

"Thank you for tonight. For the weekend. You made my trip home more than tolerable."

"Thank *you*." Her voice cracked. "It was fun." *Damn it.* Ella prayed he couldn't hear the threat of tears in her words. She wanted to be casual, as if she were the type of woman who did this all the time and that it hadn't mattered to her.

"I want to see you again."

She shook her head. "As I said, this was fun. But no. I'm sorry."

"Sorry?"

"I agree that this was a great weekend. Let's leave it at that."

"It's more than that. You know it." He wound a lock of her hair around his finger. "We have a connection."

"It doesn't matter. It can't happen again." She wouldn't let it. Already she was fracturing, barely able to hold her fragile emotions together.

"Having a connection sure as fuck means something. At least to me it does." His voice was tight, irritation punctuating his words.

"I didn't mean to insult you."

"Yeah. You did. You were trying to put distance between us. I won't let you."

"Pierce." She lifted her hand to touch his wrist but dropped it back to her side. "I've been nothing but honest. I'm looking for a relationship. I need someone who will be around, who will sleep with me, stay the night, create a future. You understood that. We both did," she added the last part to remind herself.

"How about one who lights up your ass? How about one who leaves stripes across your thighs? Or crops your pussy and inflicts the right kind of pain to make you scream out an orgasm? Who fucks you in the backseat? Who gives you memories? That's not worth something?"

Because she couldn't resist the allure, she pleaded, "Don't."

"So that's it? Your fear of being hurt is worse than your fear of taking a chance?"

She squared her shoulders. "Take a chance? With someone who's leaving in a couple of hours? Who goes on missions so top secret no one knows what he does or where he lives? People think you do some kind of administrative work, that your biggest concern is a paper cut."

He loosened her hair with slow revolutions of his finger.

"I'm not ready to move to an army base."

"I don't live on post."

"That's not the point." She exhaled. "An army town where I don't know anyone, where I don't have a job, or support network. There's a lot of women who do that, and I admire them. But I think they're stronger than I am."

"You may be underestimating yourself."

"No." She shook her head. "I can't live in a new town where I'd be alone half the time. I can't. More, I don't want to. So where would that leave us? I'd stay here in Colorado and you'd visit every few years? I guess we'd have text messaging, or phone conversations, maybe video calls. But that's not a substitute for you being with me in person." When she was even more attached to him? When she had even more experiences to forget?

"What would it take?"

This was why she shouldn't have come to the party. He was so much easier to resist if she wasn't looking at him, seeing how handsome he was, remembering the feel of the cane punishing her skin while she was mesmerized by his stunning blue eyes. "It's impossible," she said, wishing it were anything but. "A relationship takes a lot of work and commitment from two people. You are not in a place to be involved with someone like me. I'm ready to settle down. I want the whole thing. A commitment. Marriage. Stability...a mortgage. I want someone I can share goals with and a companion who will go out with me on Saturday mornings for coffee and maybe a walk." All of the things he wasn't offering.

If she waited for him, she wouldn't be meeting new people, a solid man who was also looking for companionship and a future.

But what about the sex? Or the way she had connected with Pierce? That, she knew, didn't happen often in a relationship.

"Say you'll at least talk to me, answer my texts?"

"I can't. You'd be relentless." She knew her limitations. He'd wear her down.

He grinned. "Yeah. It's a text. What harm could come from that?"

She gave a half-smile, recognizing his tease from earlier when he'd asked.

Maybe she could, after some time had passed, after she'd sorted her life out again. "Not immediately."

"You've got a lot of resolve, Ella. You're tough."

"I never said otherwise." She brought up her chin a notch and reminded him, "I've been nothing but honest."

"It wasn't a criticism."

"No?"

"Tough is good. I admire your resolve. I might not like it, but I respect it."

Tears stung her eyes, and she fought them back.

"And I like the way you take the beating you ask for."

"Now you're not playing fair." She recalled his tactic to get rid of Morgan.

"Never do. Especially when I want something."

The success of Operation Fuck Ella Senseless at the Party was proof of that. "Am I the first person to tell you no?"

"And the last."

"If you'll excuse me?" She straightened her spine and retreated behind her business façade. "Safe travels."

"I can't change your mind?"

"Please don't try."

He stepped back and she dashed past him. Though, with his superfast reflexes, she knew he'd allowed her to.

She pushed the start button and the engine kicked into life.

He took three steps away, and she glanced in her mirrors, even though she knew there was no traffic. She eased onto the dirt road.

Pierce didn't budge. He was still there when she rounded the corner. Within seconds, the house faded from sight.

At the next stop sign, she dropped her forehead to the steering wheel and gave in to the tears.

He might believe she had untapped strength. She didn't. The truth was, she was a coward. But he had been one hundred percent correct when he'd guessed that her fear of being hurt was worse than her fear of taking a chance.

The trouble was, even though they'd only been together a short amount of time, she hadn't escaped unscathed.

Chapter Seven

Pierce remained in place, watching until Ella's tail lights faded from sight. Then, instead of moving, he stared into the night and listened to the distant rumble of the car.

How in the hell had their evening gone so wrong?

The backseat car sex had been smoking. Afterward, they'd been intimate, laughing, enjoying each other's company. Operation Fuck Ella Senseless at the Party had been a success. He was confident she'd enjoyed it as much as he had. Then all of a sudden, when he'd let her know how much she mattered to him, it was as if she'd embraced her inner ice princess to push him away.

He knew one thing for sure. Ella had run because she wanted him. That wasn't ego. It was an observation of the emotion expressed in her eyes, the ferocity with which she'd held on to him when they'd been making love.

He'd spent his entire life secure, confident, never questioning a decision. He decided what he wanted and pursued it.

And now? He didn't know what the hell to do.

He refused to tell her that he was considering taking a job with Logan. There were still too many uncertainties, and he didn't want her to expect something until he was certain it would happen. He wasn't sure he could live with her disappointment.

He wished he had words that would to encourage her to stay, let him pursue her, give them a chance.

Fuck. Even if he did take the job with Logan, Pierce wasn't convinced she'd want him, anyway. She thought she wanted someone solid and stable — an accountant, maybe? Or a salesman with regular hours? Not an EMT or firefighter or even an IT guy, though. They worked hours that might not mesh with her imagined, perfect schedule.

If she got what she wanted, he suspected she'd be restless.

Ella Gibson was an intriguing mixture of innocence and defiance. All of her emotions danced in her eyes. He could read her secrets. She had a wild side, loved having her ass spanked and her limits pushed. Even though she might not admit it, she was willing to take risks.

No doubt she'd been burned by her ex. But that didn't mean all military guys — or any man who worked more than nine-to-five with two weeks of vacation a year — were unreliable, a cheater or worse.

So how the hell was he going to convince her to take a chance on him? On them? Because he could never be the man she thought she wanted.

He massaged the back of his neck.

When it was obvious she wasn't returning, despite the ridiculous hope he harbored, he walked to his car.

Mindful of appearances and not wanting to behave in a way that would risk Ella's reputation, he tucked in his shirt, shrugged into his suit jacket then replaced his tie. His belt reminded him of her. He held it, allowing himself to remember the way he'd used it on her flawless skin and the way she'd responded.

Pierce fantasized now about laying it across her flawless skin while she writhed and begged for more even as he secured a promise from her that she'd never walk away from him again.

With that satisfying image in mind, he fed the leather through the loops then fastened the buckle that had warmed from his touch.

He returned to the party as the band was packing up. The bartender was loading bottles into a container. A few people were seated at the remaining tables, talking, in no hurry to leave. His mother and father were huddled with another couple near the patio. Farrah, Bon Bon and Walter snoozed on a patch of grass near the empty tent.

Fifi trotted over and followed him to the waterfall. The bottle he'd left there earlier was still perched on a rock, and he picked it up.

He heard the click of heels on stone as someone approached, and he glanced up a second before Morgan waltzed into view. She was heading his way.

"Is there something you want to tell me?"

"About?"

"Ella."

"Ella who?"

"You're not as smart as you think you are."

"Oh?"

"Earlier this afternoon, I knew Mom didn't want me. So that was a ploy for you to be alone with Ella. I want to know what happened last night after I left the bar."

"Why would you assume anything did?"

"Oh, for crying out loud." She rolled her eyes. "I saw you looking at her."

"I was looking at plenty of women."

"Not like that. And you stayed at the Neon Moon even after I left. I don't need to be a mathematician to know that two plus two equals four. Start talking."

"Morgan, don't you have someone else to bother? Aren't you supposed to be a hostess or something?"

"My duties are all but over. So I have time for you."

"Let me be a little more precise. There's nothing to know, nothing to discuss. We can change the subject or you can scram."

"Oh, my God." She grabbed for her necklace.

"What?"

"You...you've got a thing for Ella."

He remained silent.

Her mouth formed a perfect, stunned O. "My best friend. And my brother? This is not happening. This is *so* not happening. Tell, me, Pierce. Tell me this isn't really happening."

"Okay. This is not happening."

With a scowl, she said, "You can't even look me in the eye."

He finished his water then twisted the cap back on before giving her his full attention.

"Aha."

"Aha, what?"

"You're lying."

"And?" He took aim with the bottle, lobbed it at a recycle can and scored on a bank shot. "What do you want me to say?"

"How serious is it?"

"Darling, annoying, persistent sister, I wish you still had pigtails for me to pull. You're getting nothing out of me. My private life is private."

"Oh, Pierce. You do know she's looking for something serious. A relationship with someone who isn't in the military."

"So I've learned."

"Oh, my God. You're in love with her." She placed her fingers on his sleeve. "What are you going to do?" she asked.

"Have you always been so nosy?"

"Isn't that what little sisters are good for?"

"Go bother someone else. I think Mom—"

"I'm not falling for it twice. Nice try." Nevertheless, she dropped her hand. "Are you heading back home?"

"Yeah."

"To drink hemlock?"

Or formulate a new action plan. "You can come visit me in North Carolina."

"Have you washed that pile of dishes yet?"

That had been a unique experience. He'd been deployed without warning, so fast that he hadn't cleaned the kitchen, made the bed, emptied the refrigerator. The trash, thank God, he'd remembered. But she'd shown up before he'd arrived home, and he'd spent the first twenty-four hours of her visit asleep in his clothes and shoes. "I'll hire a housekeeping service."

"Then I'll definitely consider it."

"Let me know when."

"Can I bring a guest?"

"Quit meddling."

She smiled wide, bright, as if she were an angel.

"Call if you need anything. Do me a favor? Keep an eye on Dad. Let me know if you think anything is odd."

"Come on, Pierce. There's always something odd about Dad."

He lifted a shoulder in a half-shrug. "Maybe ask Mom." Though he doubted she'd say anything. Despite the fact she didn't like him half the time, she never said anything negative about him to other people.

"And let me know if I can do anything for you...with Ella."

"Who?"

"You really are an asshole."

But that didn't stop her from falling into his arms for a hug.

"I'm going to miss you."

"My welcome mat is always out for you."

She pulled away and he saw a telltale sheen of tears in her eyes, so like his own. "I'm warning you."

"No one cries over jerks, Pierce." She swiped the back of her hand across her eyes.

"Call or text." He knew she would. Before he made it home, if his guess was right. Now if Ella would do the same...

But she'd made it clear that any contact had to come from him. Even then, she might not respond.

He started to walk away then stopped, turned back, met his little sister's gaze. "Stay out of it."

"Stay out of what?" she returned, her voice full of sass.

The couple who had been talking to his parents said their goodnights and went into the house. Since he needed to get to the airport, Pierce shook his head and pulled back his shoulders.

He joined his parents and gave his mother an air kiss. Fifi trotted over for a pet so that she wouldn't be left out. Walter cracked one eyelid and remained where he was.

"Your bedroom is always ready for you," Laurel said. "Please come home again."

He shook his father's hand. Throughout the night, he'd glanced over at Gerard. While Laurel had smiled and laughed as the belle of the ball, Gerard had been reserved. Pierce realized he might be suspicious because he was an untrusting soul, but he'd also been puzzled by Harold's behavior. The VP of Accounting at his father's headquarters had sat with him and Ella for almost an hour, dominating the conversation. If Pierce hadn't cut a getaway, they might still be there. "If you need anything, you have my number."

"Oh, no!" Laurel headed for the bar and Walter jumped up to chase her. "I need a wine before you close up."

"Of course, Mrs. Holden. Red or white?"

"A chardonnay, please."

Once they were out of earshot, Pierce leveled a look at his father. "I mean it."

"There's nothing for you to concern yourself with."

Gerard gave a tight nod. But he had no intention of ignoring his father's secretive behavior. Pierce might have to be the one to initiate phone calls and establish some sort of relationship. "I have a plane to catch."

"Goodnight." Without any further response, Gerard strode away.

Pierce took out his keys as he left the house. Another successful visit home. It had gone about as well as he'd expected. The highlight had been Ella.

How was it possible she had gotten to him so fast? He would have insisted that no woman had enough power to make him consider changing the course of his life. But now, he was obsessed with thoughts… about her, a potential future, how to get what he wanted.

Morgan was more right than she realized. He'd fallen in love with Ella.

Fuck.

His mind reeled, knocked sideways by a blow he'd never seen coming.

So now what?

Pierce opened the car door then slid behind the driver's seat.

He smelled sex and remembered being deep inside Ella, making to love to her, claiming her.

He refused to let her go.

She had been honest with him from the beginning, but part of him hadn't wanted to believe she wouldn't yield. To him, the course of action was obvious. She should move to North Carolina. Having her to come home to would be mind-blowing. It would give him focus, ground him, get him through.

Hell, he'd have even compromised and let her stay in Colorado while he worked out his future. He'd make damn sure they spent plenty of time together. Flights weren't cheap, but that wasn't insurmountable, since it was a short-term problem.

But she'd refused to yield to him.

Pierce was left with only with one mission and one outcome. Pursuit and capture. Good thing his training had left him competent at both. Operation Fuck Ella Senseless at the Party had morphed into Operation Woo Ella and Keep Her Forever.

* * * *

Ella swirled a piece of pasta in cream sauce, twirling the fork around and around, staring at the pattern it left behind.

"Who is he?"

Jolted, she looked up and across the restaurant table at her mother. The question shouldn't have surprised her. Her mother knew everything about her, always had.

Despite the fact it was a Sunday, Ella had thrown back the covers and crawled out of bed at four-thirty, disoriented and shaking. She'd had horrible nightmares of her father and Pierce, of loss and grief. Images of the two of them had intertwined, their features blending until they had been indistinguishable.

Desperate to touch them, to hold on, she'd reached a hand toward their blurred images. They'd morphed into grotesque smiles. She'd screamed as they'd vanished.

She'd returned to reality with a start, shaking and drenched in a cold sweat.

Unable to breathe, she'd climbed from bed and brewed a pot of coffee. When the first strong cup hadn't cleared the cobweb-like remnants of the dream from her psyche, she'd gone for a brisk walk around the neighborhood. Even that hadn't helped.

No matter how great the sex had been or how much she'd enjoyed his kisses and being in his arms for a dance, she was glad she'd refused to continue seeing him. There was little doubt in her mind that brutal dreams would be commonplace whenever he was deployed.

Around six a.m., he'd sent her a text message.

Since they didn't have a relationship, she'd ignored it. But she'd exhaled in relief, and she hated that she was grateful he'd thought of her.

At home, she'd drunk more coffee and watched endless episodes of television on a home improvement channel. Her gaze had been drawn to the picture of her and her father. Today, more than any time in the last twenty years, his absence tormented her.

With a sigh, she'd turned off the TV and decided to grab the vacuum and clean. As she'd walked around the house, straightening the coffee table, pushing in the barstools, making the bed, memories of Pierce had become more vibrant...and painful.

At eight, she'd texted her mom to see if she was available for lunch. Driving to Colorado Springs would take forty-five minutes to an hour and keep her from reaching for the phone.

Rather than soothing her, though, the journey had given her too much time to think. Turning up the radio hadn't worked.

"Ella?"

"How do you know the problem is a man?"

"You order carbs with a side of carbs and a glass of white wine when you have career or man trouble."

"Do I?" She looked at the food in front of her. Fettuccini alfredo and a second loaf of bread. Her water was untouched, but she had finished half of her glass of chardonnay.

"Last time we were here, you had a salad and a mineral water. If it was something to do with your job, you would have spilled it right away. So that makes me think you're having man trouble."

"Pierce Holden."

"Morgan's older brother? Didn't he bring you home one night when you were in high school and had been drinking at a party?"

"To be fair, we didn't know someone had put rum in the punch. But, yes." Even back then, he'd been a hero of sorts. Knowing her mother wouldn't judge her, she gave a complete synopsis of the weekend, except for the juiciest details.

"So what are you going to do?" Shirley took a sip of wine and sat back.

"Mope. Sulk. What else is there to do?"

"Move to North Carolina. Find out for yourself. Perhaps it won't work." She lifted one shoulder. "But then again, maybe it will. There's one way to find out."

Ella dropped her fork. She stared at her mother in open-mouthed shock. "I'm beginning to think the whole world has gone mad."

"Oh?"

"I don't know him."

"You know what kind of person he is. If he thinks enough of you to invite you to move in, there's a connection there." Shirley took one more sip. "The fact you're sitting here tells me that you're in agony. If you didn't care about him, you wouldn't be talking to me."

"I have a job."

"There are jobs in North Carolina."

"Mom. I have a house."

"Sell it. Rent it out. Or keep making the payments and keep it as an escape route in case you're right."

She blew out a breath that made a stray lock of hair flutter. "It's not that easy."

"Then go for a visit. Gather some more information before you make a decision."

With her fingertip, Ella made tiny circles on the tablecloth.

"What else is bothering you?"

"He's in the military."

"And?"

"It's some sort of super-secret, doesn't-exist-on-paper kind of thing. He lets most people think he's an admin geek. But he's not."

"That's a lot to consider."

"I don't want to go through that." She pushed her plate back. "Being alone would drive me crazy. I have no friends out there, no support system. No mom."

"It would be a big change, scary. You don't know how to make friends or live on your own. You can't make phone calls or video chat with me or Morgan or your other friends. And you'll never get another job. You're right. Move on. Go on a date with someone else tomorrow. Forget him."

"Mom!"

"Ridiculous, right?" Shirley grinned. "Made my point."

Ella tore off a piece of bread and dipped it in olive oil. "It's more than all that. I'm scared to lose him."

"I know." Shirley gave a wan smile. And when she continued, her voice was soft with heartfelt emotion. "Life doesn't come with guarantees, you know that. Just because someone is a manager in some building downtown, it doesn't mean that a freak accident won't happen. Even if I had known how things would turn out with your dad, I would have married him anyway. But I would also have savored the good times more, laughed, skipped the housework, not spent as much time worrying, fought less."

"Even with the hurt, it was worthwhile?"

"Every moment. To feel that kind of love in my lifetime? To wear his ring? See him smiling at the altar as he waited for me? To fight the demons of life together? Hold my hand as our precious daughter entered the world? *Every* moment."

Her mother's words added to her confusion about her determination to stay away from him. Ella wasn't sure she appreciated it. So she ordered chocolate cake for dessert.

"Have you heard from him since he left?"

She nodded. "He let me know he was home safe."

On the table next to her, the phone vibrated, dancing around on the white tablecloth.

"Is it Pierce?"

"No idea." To avoid temptation, Ella turned the device upside down. Since part of the reason she had driven to Colorado Springs was to shake off the upheaval of the last couple of days, she smiled at her mom. "Update me on you."

Shirley launched into tales about an airline pilot she was dating. "He's a silver fox."

And she'd made a picture of him—shirtless—her screensaver.

"What about the other guys you're involved with?"

"I change the background when I'm with them. Flowers." She laughed. "That he gave me."

"This sounds serious."

"Not at all. I just like staring at him. And having sex."

"God. Tell me you're using..." She blushed. "Condoms."

"Cherry flavored. Extra-large."

"God. Mother."

"I'm kidding. They're magnum sized."

"I need bleach for my ears." But her mother's outrageousness was the balm she needed for her soul. For an hour, a blessed hour, she was able to forget about Pierce. Until she returned to her car and looked at the phone.

When you masturbate, think of me.

Damn him. Of course she would.

Ella told herself to block his number, remove it from her directory and forget about him. She swiped the key to open his contact information. Before her courage could fail her, she selected the correct box. *Contact will be blocked. Continue?*

Her resolve fled. The pain of not knowing whether or not he was trying to reach her, whether or not he was in the country, whether he was alive and okay, was greater than the agony of ignoring him.

She pushed the red cross then deleted the message. Then she removed his phone number from her contacts to avoid the temptation of responding later.

Proud of her accomplishment, Ella dropped her phone into her purse.

As Ella drove home, her mother's words replayed. The ones about the silver fox and his condom size, Ella put in a mental incinerator, never to be thought of again.

But Ella considered the ones about Pierce.

By the time she arrived in Parker, thoughts of him crawled through her mind and heart.

When she was at home, Pierce texted again.

Even though she'd deleted his information, his name and number showed up.

She sighed.

This time there was a winking emoji and nothing else.

The man made certain she couldn't ignore him or dislike him.

Later, mentally exhausted, she took a bath.

And that night, when she couldn't get to sleep, she looked in the mirror at her ass. The tiny red mark he'd left had almost gone. But the sensation of it still seared.

She took out her vibrator and climbed into the bed.

Even though a million emotional and sixteen hundred physical miles separated them, she fantasized about Pierce and his belt—warm from his body—leaving his mark on her.

Chapter Eight

I've been thinking about having you in the Holden Holy Hell position.

Oh, God...

Ella dropped her phone. It bounced off her planner and thumped onto her desktop.

Pierce.

It had been mid-May when she'd seen him, which was more than two months ago. Three weeks ago, he'd texted to say he'd be in touch as soon as he could. He'd provided no details about when he'd be back, where he was going, what he was doing.

For agonizing days that had dragged into weeks, her phone had been silent, more noticeable since he'd left voice mails and sent texts at least every eight hours before that last message.

Since the last time he'd contacted her, she'd driven herself crazy, wondering whether he was deployed, when he might be back, not knowing whether he was safe or even in the country.

Relief that he was okay careened through her and she almost typed a response.

But the realization she'd go through this often in the future if she responded made her leave the phone where it was.

Her phone dinged again. She considered ignoring it.

No matter how many times she told herself to do just that, her fingers and curiosity overrode her brain's orders. Relief flooded her when she saw the message was from Morgan.

You're coming to a meeting of the Carpe Diem Divas. Happy hour. Tonight. No excuses or I will drag your ass out of your house. Fiesta Olé! I-25 and Arapahoe. Five o'clock. And this is happy hour. Happy hour. Which means you have to act happy. For an hour.

Ella grinned. There were times she wasn't sure whether to hug Morgan or to smother her with a pillow. There was no doubt she and Pierce were siblings.

Before Ella could come up with an excuse to decline, her phone lit up again.

p.s. I know where you live, and I have a key. I will come get your ass. So do NOT even think about going home after work like you did last time.

Ella knew that seeing her friends would be good for her. She'd spent too much time at home recently watching Netflix and eating ice cream.

After replying that she'd be there, she grabbed several packets of information about the facility and catering options then went up front to wait for a future bride and groom and mother-of-the-bride to show them the room they'd be using if they selected the country club for their wedding reception. Having the bride's mother along always made these visits interesting, but it would help her forget about Pierce and the Holden Holy Hell position.

The appointment took longer than she'd anticipated, even though she'd budgeted extra time because there would be three people in attendance rather than the usual two, she was behind schedule when she left the office to drive to Denver to meet her friends.

When she walked into the restaurant's bar section, she discovered Morgan, Ava, Jennifer and Eden already sipping margaritas. She took the only empty chair and grinned when she saw a frozen drink at her plate, too.

She took a long drink of the sweet-and-sour beverage then shook her head at the bite from the tequila. "Is this a double?"

"No," Ava said.

"You just don't get out much," Morgan replied.

"I'm here now," Ella said. "Where's Noelle?" Though Ella wasn't an official member of the Carpe Diem Divas, she was sometimes invited when they were meeting at the south end of Denver. The Divas had started as a few friends supporting each other through recent breakups. Even though Noelle was now happily married to one of the area's renowned Doms, the group was so committed to each other that they didn't want Noelle to leave.

"She and Joe are up at their mountain house getting ready for a play party that they're having this weekend," Jennifer said. "I think Logan and I are going. Would you like to attend?"

"Uh." The invitation stunned her, but not as much as her reaction. "No." If she ever attended another club, she wanted to go with Pierce. He'd ruined her for other men. But the mention of BDSM made her squirm, remember the marks he'd given her and the orgasms that had ripped through her from his attentions. "I mean, thanks."

"Aren't you into that BDSM stuff?" Ava asked.

Jennifer pointed her straw at Ava. "It's not *that* BDSM stuff, like it's something weird. You should give it a try."

"Oh, fuck no. Ain't no man spanking this fine ass." She wriggled in her seat.

"You might like it," Morgan said.

"I'll leave that to the rest of you kinky bitches. I'm just looking for a man who likes to eat at the Y like his life depends on it. Which it might."

"Oh, my God!" Ella roared.

People from other tables glanced in their direction.

"Speaking of... How was your date last week?" Eden asked.

Ava shook her head. "Could barely introduce him to the kitty. Never did get him to pet it."

Right then, Ella decided to meet up with the Divas every chance she had.

As she was finishing the last drop of her cocktail, she became aware of Morgan's gaze on her. "What?"

"How's my brother?"

"What?"

"Pierce?" Ava demanded.

"What's this about Pierce?" Eden asked.

Blinking innocently, Morgan twirled the ice in her glass.

"Are you fishing?" Ella asked. Or had she heard something from Pierce?

"I told Pierce after the anniversary party I didn't have to be a mathematician to figure this out. I saw the way he was looking at you. And no one takes that long to walk someone to the car when they leave. And since you told me you didn't go home with Randall that Friday night, I figured that you and my brother were—"

"Randall?" Ava interrupted to stare across at Ella. "You were going to go home with"—she plugged her nose so that her voice had an upper crust, hoity-toity air—"Randall W. Thurston, Jr.?"

"No." Ella shook her head.

"You might have if Pierce hadn't put a stop to it."

"He's banned from Joe and Noelle's parties," Jennifer added. "Did you know that?"

Morgan replied for both of them, "Pierce told us."

Ava's eyes widened. "What does Pierce know about that? Is he a kinkster?"

Everyone fell silent and looked at Ella. "How would I know?"

"Tell us something." Morgan wrinkled her nose. "Anything."

"There's nothing to say. If you want more than that, you'll need to ask Pierce."

"Checkmate. He said to ask you."

Eden leaned forward. "I'm dying to know."

"There's nothing to tell. You all know I don't date men unless they're marriage material. And he lives in North Carolina."

Jennifer scowled. "Isn't he moving to Colorado?"

The bottom dropped out of Ella's heart. "What?" Her ears rang and the tequila soured in her stomach.

"He's been talking to Logan about joining the detective agency. It won't happen right away, but I know they've been having conversations." Jennifer scowled. "Shit, shit, shit. That's not a secret, is it?"

"I didn't know," Morgan said, her hand frozen in place.

Ella was too stunned to say anything.

"I must have misunderstood something," Jennifer rushed to say. "At any rate, I apologize for opening my big mouth." Her hand shook. "I'm going to be in trouble for this one. Repeating privileged information. All of a sudden, I'm not quite as excited about going home tonight. Confession may be good for the soul, but it's hell on my butt."

"I don't think you need to say anything to Logan," Eden said, always the loyal one. "You didn't know it was a secret."

"He'll find out. No doubt. And hiding it will make it more difficult for me to sit down when he does."

"You couldn't have known," Morgan reassured Jennifer. "None of us will say anything."

Conversation went on around Ella, like insects droning in her ears, but she didn't respond to any of it.

If he cared about her, wouldn't he have mentioned something so important?

A more rational part of her brain couldn't blame him. She hadn't replied to his numerous texts. Of course he wouldn't share intimate details of his life.

The server arrived with the bill and Jennifer picked it up, saying, "It's the least I can do for ruining everyone's evening."

"You didn't ruin anything," Eden assured her.

"I'll pay next time," Ava promised.

"I'm going to kick his sorry soul into the next zip code when I see him," Morgan said. "He hasn't said a word to Mom or Dad, either."

The gathering broke up, and Morgan walked outside with Ella.

"Ella. I'm sorry. I had no idea what I was starting," Morgan apologized. "I wanted to get you out, have some fun, maybe learn some salacious details about my brother. But I had no intention of hurting you."

"He has sent me text messages and called me a few times since he went back to Fort Bragg, but I've never answered." The small disclosure was as much as she would reveal. "But Jennifer's announcement is news to me. He said nothing."

"He can be an ass at times." Morgan stopped near her car. "He must have wanted it to be a surprise."

"Well, it worked."

"He cares about you. I know it."

Ella gave a brave smile that she was afraid would shatter. "We're friends. Nothing more."

"I hate him a little right now."

"Don't." Ella shrugged. "At least not on my behalf." She knew what she'd been doing. At least she thought she had.

"There's nothing I can say to make this better, is there?"

"I'll be fine." Though the last thing she wanted was company or obligations, Ella wanted to make Morgan feel better. "Let's have happy hour again next week."

"Same place and time?"

"The margaritas are good." Ella nodded.

"Call me if you want to talk or go out or go shopping. Or anything."

"I will." That part was a lie.

When she was in the car, Ella looked at her phone.

The screen was blank.

She wished she had been surprised.

* * * *

At work the next afternoon, Ella's desk phone buzzed. From the extension on the display, she knew it was from the receptionist at the podium.

"Hey, Ella. I've got a gentleman who'd like to talk to someone about membership. And Barb left about twenty minutes ago."

"I'll be right there."

Typically, potential members scheduled an appointment in advance. Barb would show them the facility and sometimes treat them to a meal or a beverage in the bar. Every once in a while, someone would show up without calling, and on those occasions, the club provided information and encouraged the visitor to return for an official tour.

She shrugged into her black blazer and took a vanity second to look in the mirror to ensure she didn't need to dab on some eye cream. She hadn't slept well last night, waiting for Pierce to text and say something. Anything. But he never had.

Deciding she wouldn't frighten the visitor, she grabbed a folder filled with informational material. Then she pasted a practiced smile on her lips as she walked through the public areas of the club toward the podium.

She missed a step when she saw Pierce in the lobby. He was so handsome in a polo shirt, navy slacks and a blazer that her breath lodged in her throat.

"Ella, this is Mr. Holden," the receptionist said.

Unable to speak, she nodded.

Since he extended his hand, she had no option but to accept it, even though every instinct warned her not to.

Instinct had been right.

His grip was reassuring, promising, strong, and most of all, welcomed by the most feminine part of her. The one that was unable to resist him.

She extracted her hand faster than was polite. "Staff Sergeant Holden, is it? Rather than Mr. Holden?"

The receptionist turned to greet a couple of ladies dressed for tea.

"It is."

Had Jennifer been wrong last night? And what was he doing here? Her knees knocked together, and she forced herself to stand up straight. "I'm sure you heard that Barb, who handles new memberships, isn't available? You're welcome to come back for a formal tour of the premises. In the meantime, I'm happy to answer any questions you might have."

In response, he dropped to one knee. Her mouth opened and heat flooded her body.

The receptionist, and the ladies who were there for afternoon tea, all turned to stare.

"Pierce?"

"I do have a question, Ella." His eyes were brighter, more intense than she'd ever seen, and a serious frown had settled between his brows.

He reached into his pocket and pulled out a ring box. She lost her grip on the folder and it fell to the floor.

"Will you marry me?"

"What?"

Instead of responding, he opened the box.

The princess-cut diamond was ginormous, the overhead lighting bouncing off its brilliance and refracting all the colors of the rainbow.

"I don't understand."

"You made your position clear. I want you. I will do whatever it takes to deserve you. It will take some compromise from you, because it will be a while until I get my official discharge. I'm transferring to Fort Carson. That's the closest I can get to you. And I've made post-retirement plans to work with Logan Powell in his detective agency. So we have a lot of decisions to make. About where to live, how to manage your doubts. Things won't be perfect for a long time. I shouldn't have to deploy, but if I do, we'll get through it together." He took a breath, but not long enough for her to respond before he continued. "No doubt you'll have issues with me working with Logan, but we'll deal with that, too. Together. This is everything I have to offer you, Ella. Please tell me it's enough, that you're willing to try as hard as I am. Freaking yield a little. I'm begging you."

Words failed her and emotion flooded her.

"I love you, Ella. It took me some time to wake up to that fact. And I was frustrated that you wouldn't give in or compromise. Being away from you, knowing I couldn't talk to you and that you wouldn't respond to any of my texts, made me a madman."

One of the ladies fanned herself.

"Okay. Now say something. Anything."

"I…" She wished she could. But all of her dreams — of being with a fantastic person, a caring Dominant, someone who would support her and push her — were right there. It thrilled and overwhelmed her.

"Put me out of my misery, Ella, please. This is my new version of the Holden Holy Hell position."

Tears spilled from her eyes, and she laughed through them.

"Is that a yes?"

"Yes!"

He pulled the ring from the box, and the two ladies clapped.

Her future husband slid the ring on her finger.

It looked like hope and promise rolled into one.

"You're mine." Then he stood and raised her hand and kissed it. "I'd planned to come to your house tonight, but I couldn't wait."

"I'm glad."

The ladies and the receptionist came over to shake hands, give hugs and share their best wishes.

Then he backed her into a portico. "We can't," she protested when the wall prevented her from moving any farther.

"The fuck we can't. I braved IEDs and the entire might of the US military to get to you, red tape, bureaucratic bullshit, then airplane reservations, rental cars. If you don't think I'm kissing my future bride—"

"You'll get me fired!"

"Good. That will give you the opportunity to practice being my sex slave. I'll teach you a few more of my favorite positions."

She giggled. "When you put it that way..." She tried to glance around, but he captured her chin and imprisoned her.

"Open your mouth."

"Yes, Sir," she whispered. Ella breathed him in, the scent of determination and sexual charisma. Her body vibrated with recognition that he was the man she'd been waiting for her whole life. He cared enough about her to make big changes to his career and future to accommodate her. It wasn't a perfect solution, but it was better than she'd dared hope for.

Thrilled, nervous at the idea of being caught, she leaned into him, wrapping her arms around his neck so that she could look at him and her engagement ring.

He claimed her mouth, took what was his, everything she had to offer.

His mouth was hot and he telegraphed sensual need. "I've got to get you home."

Everything he wanted, she did, too. "I can leave in about an hour."

He glowered.

She might have laughed at his expression if she weren't afraid he'd toss her over his shoulder and carry her out of the front door. "I'll see if someone will cover for me."

"I'll meet you at your place?"

"Perfect."

Ella's boss allowed her to go home early to celebrate, and within half an hour, she was pulling into the driveway at her townhouse, heart pounding, anticipating what was ahead.

He was lazing against the hood of his rental car, somehow managing to look badass even though he was dressed for the country club.

He pushed away, strode over to her, opened her door then helped her out.

"You're more beautiful every time I see you."

He always took her breath away.

"Let's start this relationship the right way." His voice was edged with dominance, and corresponding pleasure rushed through her, making her clit throb.

"Sir?"

He held out his hand for her keys, and she tossed them to him.

Before she knew what he was about, he had her off the ground and over his shoulder. Breath whooshed out of her.

"Carrying you across the threshold."

"That's not how it works," she protested, kicking.

"It does in this relationship." With a flick of his hand, he closed the car door.

"Pierce! Put me down!"

Instead, he brushed her skirt up a little and gave her ass a hard spank.

She melted. He understood her so completely, perfectly.

He was worth the wait.

His steps were long and confident as he walked to the house, unlocked and opened the door. After he carried her inside, he kicked it closed behind them.

"It's time for you to learn the Holden-Gibson Forever pose," he said, lowering her to the floor. "Shall we get started?"

"Oh, Sir. I thought you'd never ask."

Chapter Nine

"Put down your purse and come here, Ella. You're not quite ready to leave."

At the implacable tone in Pierce's voice, her heart leaped then settled into a wild gallop. She turned to look at Pierce, her Dom, her fiancé, her world. He was holding a butt plug unlike any she'd ever seen. Her tummy plunged. The thing was gorgeous. A work of art. It was crafted from glass with a stunning spiral of deep blue sneaking up the interior. It was also gigantic. At its thickest, it had to be twice the size of the biggest one they'd ever used. And even the stem was much thicker than she was accustomed to. There was no way her sphincter would adjust to that monster, no matter how long she was forced to wear it.

Some part of her should have expected his order. Pierce often stunned her with the unexpected, keeping their relationship fresh.

The past two months had been difficult. She'd flown to North Carolina to spend some time with him and help him pack his belongings. He'd shipped most of his personal items to her townhome since he would be living temporarily in barracks at Fort Carson. Their time together while they waited for his discharge to be processed was limited. Every reunion, though, deepened her love for him. And she was becoming addicted to his dominance. Or had been. Until this moment. "Uhm…"

"Do I need to tell you twice?"

"No, Sir. But…" She trailed off. "The size of that thing. And, aren't we pressed for time? I mean, with traffic, we might be late. I hate to keep Morgan waiting."

"We'll be later with each second that you stall."

"Pierce…"

He didn't say anything. Instead, he remained where he was, watching her squirm. And damn him, he looked so handsome in an athletic-fitting T-shirt that showed his lean runner's physique. She had a rush of sexual hunger every time she saw him.

"Ella? You're stalling. That won't go well for you."

"Maybe we should put it in after we get home." And she had a chance to distract him and make him forget the enormous thing existed.

"We could do that."

She smiled. Then she exhaled a breath she hadn't known she was holding.

"But we're not going to."

Ella glanced back toward the door, making certain he understood her preference to leave. But the frustrating man didn't budge or acknowledge her wishes. "That thing is bigger than your cock." It wasn't. But it intimidated her nevertheless.

"I could stretch you out with my dick first, if that puts your mind at ease?"

"No!" They hadn't done that yet, and she was in no hurry to do so. Small plugs were enough for her.

He grinned. "Then get your ass over here, sub."

After releasing her grip on her purse, she walked to him.

Pierce placed the plug on the coffee table next to a bottle of lube before removing the bottom cushion from the couch so that the fabric-covered frame was exposed. "Squat on the edge here."

"Have you lost your mind? What if I go through that material?"

"Your weight will be on the edge, on the steel frame. You won't be anywhere near the middle. The couch and your hot little body will both be safe."

In true Dom style, he said no more. He'd responded to her objections, but he didn't argue or cajole or invite questions. Instead, he waited for her compliance.

She stood there, contemplating. But she knew he wouldn't relent.

With a sigh, she kicked off her shoes then wriggled out of her panties. "Shall I take off my dress?"

"No."

Out of reasons to stall, she climbed onto the couch then lowered herself into the awkward position he'd said.

"Come my direction a bit more."

"I will fall off."

"You won't. Spread your knees to shoulder-width, then put your weight on the balls of your feet on the edge to help. You can hold onto the back for balance."

"Is this another version of the Holden Reverse Half Squat?" She realized there was nothing *half* about it.

"There are a number of modifications I've been thinking of. Keeps me awake at night. But I will tell you this, I like having your pussy and ass available for my use like this. You're vulnerable."

"Because my life is at risk."

"I've heard enough." He snatched her panties from the floor, wadded them. "Open."

"But..."

Pierce seized the opportunity to shove the lacy material deep into her mouth. Then he took hold of her chin and turned her to face him.

God, how she had missed him when he'd been gone. His gaze bored into hers, his deep blue eyes compelling her not to look away.

"This is going up your ass and you're going to be a good girl and take the whole thing without complaint. And at dinner, I'm going to find the hardest chair in the restaurant and force you to sit flat so that it's driven high inside you. Every time you move or breathe, you will remember I'm your Dom."

Even though the plug was nowhere near her, her ass cheeks clenched.

"I will enjoy watching you suffer. And if you're lucky, I'll let you go into the ladies' room and masturbate."

"*Let me?*" Since her mouth was stuffed full of lace, the words were garbled.

"If you're lucky."

He lifted her dress and rolled it up to tuck the hem inside her fitted waistband. She wasn't sure how he accomplished it, but the material stayed in place.

A soft pop told her he'd opened the lid on the lube bottle. She imagined him smearing the smooth surface with the viscous liquid, and before she was ready, Pierce cupped a hand on her left shoulder to hold her in place while pressing the rounded tip against the entrance of her rear.

"*Oww.*"

"I haven't started yet. I will put it in the freezer for a few seconds if you continue to misbehave."

She shook her head frantically.

"In that case, shall we?"

Even though she hated to, she nodded.

"Bear down."

Ella sucked in a breath, and when she exhaled, he started forward with inexorable force. "*It...*" The word, even to her, was incomprehensible.

The pressure became too much, and she rocked forward, frantic to escape.

"Get back in place, if you please."

Now she just wanted to get it over with. The less time she was in agony, the better. Resolved, she deepened her squat, offering him greater access to her body.

"Such an amazing sub, princess." He began the slow, relentless torment again.

She prayed the thing was at its widest because she was certain her ass couldn't be stretched any farther.

"Almost there. Damn, I love watching it go in you. I'm not sure I'll ever use anything other than glass on you." Without warning, he let go of her shoulder to grab her hair and tug her head back. He kissed her forehead, distracting her enough that she didn't move when he pressed the plug all the way in.

She gasped. And the thing seemed to settle in. Ella sighed with relief as her muscles clamped around the post.

"Perfect. Stay there for a second." He kissed her again, and she knew she'd endure anything as long as he rewarded her with that smile and expression of pride in his eyes.

He grabbed a damp cloth that she hadn't noticed before and wiped the excess lube from her skin. "Knowing that's inside you will torture me all evening."

He helped her to stand before turning her to face him. After smoothing her dress into place, he plucked the panties from her mouth.

"Torture *you*, Sir?" She placed her hands on her hips.

"Yeah. I'm going to have a hard-on all night."

"So sorry for your anguish, Sir." She bent to slip into her panties.

Pierce grinned and offered his arm. "Shall we?"

Outside, he helped her into the car before sliding behind the wheel.

He watched her squirm as she tried to get comfortable. She tightened her ass cheeks. When that didn't help, she relaxed them. That was every bit as unsuccessful. "The plug is too big."

"Uh-huh." After checking the surroundings, he pulled from the parking spot.

"Can I have any sympathy? A single drop of kindness?"

"Nope. That will only lead to more and a request for me to allow you to take it out."

Relaxing wasn't easy.

He talked about his day and asked about hers. When his phone rang, Logan Powell's name appeared on the screen in front of them.

"Sorry. I've got to take this call."

"Go ahead."

"Holden. You're on speaker phone."

"Want me to call back later?" Logan asked.

She pulled out her phone to play with while he spoke. "No."

"There's something here. Want us to move forward? Or should we drop it?"

Ella glanced up from her screen.

A tiny muscle ticked in Pierce's jaw. "I want to see it first."

"Tonight? Tomorrow?"

"0800."

"My office." Logan ended the call.

Pierce gripped the steering wheel so hard that muscles in his forearms jumped. He drove with complete competence even though he was silent.

"Do you want to talk about it?" She slipped her phone back into her bag and focused on Pierce.

"When I was home for my parents' anniversary, my dad was acting a little…" He shook his head. "I can't describe it. I had a hunch he wanted to talk about something, but he didn't. And the way his CFO behaved at the party…"

"Maybe he was trying to tell you something?" Among the stupid jokes about pushing paper and needing an army to help them.

"So I asked Logan for his opinion. I don't know what it means. Not going to guess. But I'm going to deal with it."

"We don't have to go out tonight. I can call Morgan and cancel."

He relaxed his grip. "In the army, I learned to eat when I can. Sleep at every opportunity. From you, I'm learning to enjoy life. As you said, it's important to spend time with friends as well as family. And think about fucking you and the way your ass even now is wide open because I want it to be."

She leaned to one side. "This thing with your dad is important."

"And I'll know more details tomorrow. Then I'll consult with others and decide on a course of action if necessary. Everything in due time. Nothing hurried. This could take days. Weeks. Months."

Calculated, like everything else he did.

"Please, not a word about Dad in front of Morgan. I don't want her worried. If she needs to know something, I'll inform her."

Ella nodded.

They arrived at the restaurant before Morgan.

Once they were seated at a table near the window with margaritas in front of them, he looked across at her.

"Take off your panties."

Startled, Ella glanced around the restaurant to see if anyone had overheard Pierce's outrageous order. "What?"

"You heard me."

"I did, Sir." His command caught her off guard, stunning her and shooting an illicit thrill through her body, straight to her pussy, making her tighten her grip on the plug.

"Then?"

"In the bathroom?"

"Right here. Right now."

His blue eyes blazed with uncompromising demand. She had no doubt he meant it.

Thanking the stars for the white linen tablecloth, she reached her hands beneath her dress and worked her thong over her hips and down her thighs. When she reached her knees, she hazarded a glance to be certain no one could see her then pretended to look on the floor for something as she pulled her feet from her sandals and worked the panties the rest of the way off.

When she sat up, he was smiling.

"Hand them over."

With a sigh, she wadded the material into a ball and offered them to him.

"You may be excused to the ladies' room to masturbate. I don't care whether you orgasm or not."

She knew his words were more than a suggestion. "Yes, Sir."

With his free hand, he snagged her wrist as she walked past him, forcing her to stop. "I love you, Ella."

"I love you, Sir."

He kissed her hand before releasing her.

The stalls in the ladies' room were luxurious, with floor-to-ceiling wooden louvered doors, giving her plenty of privacy. She hadn't thought she could come, but the moment she touched her clit, she groaned.

Everything he'd done—from his tone, to the gentleness of his touch, to his commands, to the oversized plug that split her apart—turned her on.

She parted her labia with her left hand and stroked her clit even harder, pretending Pierce was stimulating her. The thought of him made her close her eyes and she surrendered to the fantasy. She pressed her lips together so she didn't moan again, and she rubbed harder, faster.

So damn good.

His power over her was complete. And she loved it.

She pushed the balls of her feet down, and the angle change made the plug move. The friction on the thousands of nerve endings in her anus pushed her over the edge. She came hard. Even though she tried not to, she moaned as she dropped her head forward onto her knees.

It took her a few seconds to recover before she pulled herself together and headed for the sink to wash her hands and finger-comb her hair into some semblance of normalcy.

When she returned to the table, Morgan was there. She'd stolen Ella's margarita and stood to give her a big hug.

"I can't believe I get to see the two of you together."

Pierce stood to pull out her chair. Against her ear he said, "Sit flat on your ass, princess."

She did, shifted, then stayed still.

He never stopped watching her.

The waiter returned with another round of drinks and a basket of chips to go with a fresh bowl of salsa.

They gave Morgan all the news on the move and job situation. Ella noticed he never mentioned their parents.

Morgan looked from one to the other. "Have you set a wedding date?"

"She's stalling."

"I'm not." She scowled at him over her chip. "I want us to be settled and spend some time together before we make it permanent."

"Settled?" Morgan sat back. "When does that ever happen? I think you should set a date and figure it out."

"Same thing I keep telling her." Pierce looked at her. "You're the one who told me you wouldn't get in a relationship unless it led to marriage."

"You can't use my words against me."

Morgan grinned. "He did that."

They were probably right. Life might not get much easier when he was working for Logan. "I'll set one." She crunched her chip.

Morgan licked salt from the rim of her glass. "I'll nag you until you do."

"*That*, I believe."

They all laughed. Under the table, he touched Ella's leg above the knee.

And within an hour, they were back at home.

He closed and locked the door while she placed her purse on a nearby table.

"You masturbated at the restaurant?"

"I always do what my Dom tells me."

His pupils flared. "And did you come?"

"Right away."

He shook his head. "I have to have you."

"I would have been happy to stay at home with you all night, Sir."

He tossed his keys into a metal bowl on the table, one she'd put there for him. Maybe Morgan was right. Maybe it was time Ella set a date. In many small ways, she and Pierce were already settled into a relationship. "Next summer."

"For the wedding?"

"That will give us time to plan, reserve a venue —"

"Spoken like a person who handles events. How about we actualize our own vows in the mountains and then have a party later? No one has to know. I want you as mine, now."

"Spring."

"This winter."

She exhaled. "How about you fuck me?"

"Are you trying to distract me?"

"Is it working?"

"I have incredible focus. If it works, it would be temporary." He grinned. "Take off your dress. And crawl to the bedroom. I want to see your ass move. I want to see the plug."

As always, he gave her plenty of opportunity to shake off her self-doubts.

Ella pulled off the dress then removed her bra before lowering herself to floor.

Pierce sucked in a sharp breath, and that made her confidence soar.

Even though she blushed, she crawled to the bedroom. He followed behind, telling her how gorgeous she was.

"On the bed. On your back."

She exaggerated her motions, pretending to be a sex kitten.

After undressing in record time, he rolled on a condom and climbing onto the bed on top of her. "It's going to be tight with the plug."

"I know." But her pussy was already wet. "Fuck me, Sir."

Instead, he tormented her clit a dozen times with his tongue then said, "I want your knees on my shoulders. I want to be as deep inside you as possible."

She lifted her legs and he moved toward her, pressing his shoulders against the backs of her knees. "*This.* Yes, Sir… Exactly like this."

"God*damn.*"

His strength and power seemed to split her apart. But she took him, all of him, everything he wanted her to have, everything she needed.

He called out her name as he came, the sound broken into two distinct, guttural sounds.

Once he was replete, he didn't collapse on her. Instead, he lifted his body and looked at her. "Still need a little more?"

"The plug and the angle is...I don't know."

He toyed with her, stroking her clit, paying close attention to her.

"Pierce!"

"You're almost there."

She closed her eyes and gave herself over to the sensations. She squeezed her butt cheeks, clamping down on the plug.

Then he maneuvered his body so he could tease one of her nipples with his tongue.

"Damn." So, so close.

He bit.

She arched. He stopped biting and instead sucked hard. Then he plunged a couple of fingers into her heated pussy and flicked her clit with his thumb until she shattered from the sensual overload.

Pierce stayed there until she rode it out. She wasn't sure she'd ever be able to move again. More, she wasn't sure she wanted to.

For thirty seconds, maybe more, she floated, somewhere quiet and peaceful as her heart rate returned to normal.

When she opened her eyes, he was looking at her. He grinned. "Put your hands over your head."

It took some effort since her limbs felt wooden, but once she managed it, he clamped her wrists.

"This is my favorite version of the Holden-Gibson Forever pose. You're mine, Ella. *Mine.* To love. Nurture. Protect."

"And spank my ass?"

His blue eyes seared hers. "I wouldn't have it any other way."

"I wouldn't, either, Sir."

"Good. Then set a date." He paused. "For the wedding."

"You're relentless, Pierce. Do you ever stop?"

"You're vulnerable. I plan to take advantage of it. Next week."

"No. No. No. *No*. Next summer. June."

He continued to stare at her. "January."

"April." Before facilities got booked for proms and weddings.

"Done."

She glared at him. "Was that the date you wanted?"

He grinned.

"Did you just win? You won. That's not winning, that's cheating."

"And?"

Instead of waiting for an answer, he swooped in for a kiss so deep and thrilling and emotional that words weren't needed.

When he finally ended it, with her mouth swollen from the way he devoured her, he said, "Tell me you're not upset."

"Pierce, in all the ways that it counts, I'm already your wife. I love you."

He grinned and gave a slow, sexy, searing look that reflected his devotion.

Her insides melted. No matter what the future held, she had the confidence they would deal with it together.

"In that case, Mrs. Holden, let's get started on the honeymoon."

**Want to see more from this author?
Here's a taster for you to enjoy!**

Crave
Sierra Cartwright

Excerpt

"That's the most ridiculous thing I've ever heard you say. Spectacular in its stupidity. Borderline insane, even. You've had some idiotic moments in the last four years, but even for you, this is remarkable." He waved a hand. "What in the *hell* are you thinking?"

Sarah hadn't expected her old friend Julien to be wildly enthusiastic about her request to hook her up with her former boyfriend, but this? "Don't hold back," she returned, reaching for the bottle of wine. Like everything in Julien Bonds' life, the Merlot, a brand she'd never heard of and couldn't pronounce, was expensive.

"Sweetling, I haven't even yet begun," he said as she poured wine into her glass.

"Sweetling?"

"Better than piranha, I should think."

"Piranha?" she asked, stung. "Is that how you see me?"

"Well, you don't really have the teeth for it, do you? So I settled for sweetling."

"That doesn't fit me, either."

"You're right. I'm back to the man-eating carnivore image, then."

"Sweetling it is," she agreed.

He grinned. He'd won this skirmish, but she intended to win the bigger battle.

Glass in hand, she sat back and curled her bare legs beneath her. The white leather couch was smooth, soft, more inviting than her host. Well, that wasn't exactly true. He *had* agreed to see her, even though she'd had to accommodate his bizarre schedule and leave a party she'd been attending in northern California.

When she'd exited his private elevator, the bottle had already been uncorked and waiting. So he wasn't completely inhospitable.

Julien pressed his palms together and regarded her across his fingertips. Although it was in the ever-expanding heart of Silicon Valley, his sprawling office suite at 1, Bonds Street was every bit as eclectic as he was. The building itself was only a year old. Rather than opting for a traditional structure, Julien had instructed his team of architects to design something that looked more like a UFO than a corporate headquarters.

This portion of Julien's space was streamlined, decorated in white, chrome and glass. A shocking blood-red rug that cost at least as much as her yearly mortgage payment was splashed across the white marble floor.

Here he had no clutter, not even a magazine.

His desk was about half of a football field away. Its vast surface was covered with electronics that looked as if they were in various stages of development.

A silk-screened Chinese partition blocked off the back of the room. Behind its expanse, she knew, was a creative and frightening workspace. She'd seen it once and had been taken aback by the disaster. Papers had been scattered on every flat surface, tossed on the floor, tacked to the walls, taped to the tables, wadded and tossed in the general direction of an overflowing garbage can.

A mattress, sheathed with twelve hundred thread-count sheets, lay shoved against a wall. He kept it on hand for the times — days — that he was so involved in a project that he didn't go home.

It was a good thing his office had a shower and a closet full of suits as well as sweatpants. He could greet the President of the United States or do a presentation to the city council then go back to his slovenly and strange ways, including eating celery and peanut butter for two meals a day.

Still, he was the best sort of friend, and he had been since she'd first met him four years before. He'd had an appointment with her boss, Reece McRae, and he'd apologised for showing up early. She'd stood there, files clutched against her chest, speechless, trapped somewhere between star-struck and awestruck. But Julien had helped himself to a glass of Scotch and had told her tales of his college days with Reece.

In the hour it had taken Reece to arrive, Julien had charmed her and extracted all her secrets. Rather than turn up his nose at her financial struggle to put herself through college, he'd told her he admired her scrappy determination. She'd walked away from the meeting believing none of the nasty things said about him in the press, though he assured her that he really was an evil bastard who chewed the heads off his competitors.

Now, four years later, he'd be the first person she'd call if she needed bail money. She knew he'd insist on hearing all the gritty, salacious details before he sprang her loose. But he'd be there.

"I have to point out that there are more than seven billion people on the planet," he continued, still regarding her. "I should think at least half of them are men. Even if you discount those who are outside your age range, married or gay, I'd say you could have your choice of, at least five hundred million eligible bachelors."

"True."

"And you want one in specific."

"Yes." She took a drink of her wine. *Reece.*

About the Author

Sierra Cartwright was born in Manchester, England and raised in Colorado. Moving to the United States was nothing like her young imagination had concocted. She expected to see cowboys everywhere, and a covered wagon or two would have been really nice!

Now she writes novels as untamed as the Rockies, while spending a fair amount of time in Texas…where, it turns out, the Texas Rangers law officers don't ride horses to roundup the bad guys, or have six-shooters strapped to their sexy thighs as she expected. And she's yet to see a poster that says Wanted: Dead or Alive. (Can you tell she has a vivid imagination?)

Sierra wrote her first book at age nine, a fanfic episode of Star Trek when she was fifteen, and she completed her first romance novel at nineteen. She actually kissed William Shatner (Captain Kirk) on the cheek once, and she says that's her biggest claim to fame.

Her adventure through the turmoil of trust has taught her that love is the greatest gift. Like her image of the Old West, her writing is untamed, and nothing is off-limits.

She invites you to take a walk on the wild side…but only if you dare.

Sierral loves to hear from readers. You can find her contact information, website details and author profile page at http://www.totallybound.com.

TOTALLY
BOUND

Home of Erotic Romance

Made in the USA
Middletown, DE
23 March 2019